THE

RIVER

TO

THE

SEA

THE

RIVER

TO

THE

SEA

by

JOHN ANTROBUS

BearManor Media

2022

ACKNOWLEDGEMENTS

My thanks to Peter Embling for proof reading and layout and for generally being helpful and encouraging.

And to Ben Ohmart who inspires me to keep writing as he keeps publishing my work. And so we continue. Thanks so much, Ben.

Who else can I thank? Thanks to all who buy this book and take a journey into their own minds which is what reading is all about. Never be scared not to know. That's where the fun begins...

Published in the USA by
BearManor Media
1317 Edgewater Dr. #110
Orlando, FL 32804
www.BearManorMedia.com

Paperback edition: ISBN: 978-1-62933-932-0
Hardcover edition: ISBN: 978-1-62933-933-7

INTRODUCTION

Inspector Jack Hedge first appeared in *Invitation To A Plague*, a case the Government did not want solved involving a secret germ warfare experiment that went disastrously wrong leaking a fatal virus into the public domain and potentially across the world. In fact some spheres of influence would like the inspector dead and gone...

That novel was written in eight days pre-sobriety over fifty years ago and it lay in my files being dusted off from time to time until recently when the ever adventurous Ben Ohmart read the manuscript and offered to publish it through his company, BearManor Media. I decided it was better to let the manuscript be published pretty much as written. Now, after many years of sobriety – with a little help from my friends, as the song goes – I began writing this sequel, *The River To The Sea*, which, on and off, has taken much longer than eight days.

The earlier 'Plague' volume did succeed in an option of the film rights being bought by Apple, the Beatles company, and we even had a meeting in the basement of the Beatles shop on Baker Street (which, strewn with coat hangers, was no longer in business). Present at the meeting, lined up to play Inspector Hedge was Sean Connery. Sadly it did not happen. The option lapsed and the film is still waiting to be made.

So, here we are into today – JUST FOR TODAY – and was it ever different than that? Let's make it into something wonderful. Perhaps this book will become part of this ever-present day for you...

I am the river to the sea, said Inspector Hedge, not knowing why he had said it. Like much of what he said and did these days. He was on a journey of not knowing until suddenly one day he would know and that would be an end to that story. And the beginning of a new story...

1

A tram loomed out of the fog containing a cargo of dead souls heading for Croydon. Its bell clanged mournfully as it disappeared back into the swirling mists that shrouded the city. Inspector Hedge thought... he thought...

But then where did thinking get you?

Action was the answer. This was his beat. It was his manor. Not that he was officially an on the beat uniformed policeman any longer after his various promotions and his switch to the Met CID Plain Clothes branch. Why should that stop him from treading the sour pavements and peering into shop doorways for any lurkers? Being a bit of a presence. Wearing his uniform. Being seen. Him. He was on sick leave with time at his disposal so why not get out and meet the people and feel his boots on the ground again?

It was a run-down district much suited to foggy days, an opportunity to hide the grime-ridden facades of desperate lives in vaporous possibilities. The manor could hardly be called historic either. Everything built upon it had been cheap and cheerful jerry-building made to become obsolete like a cheap vacuum cleaner. The gaping teeth of bomb sites along the street were the only hint of improvements to come. The inspector could hardly see his hand in front of him – that hand he knew so well – so thick was the fog of the polluted coal-reeking air. He coughed and lost the pavement edge and turning a corner – if it was a corner – came up against a building. He found himself to be...

To be, yes...

or not to be...

staring into the window of a junk shop. He peered through the smeared window pane rubbing the glass with his sleeve to improve the view of objects on display...

Were his eyes deceiving him?

On a stand was set Inflatable Police Woman Doris, his old associate. Patched as she was in several places and sagging from leaked or half hearted inflation yet she stirred his heart strings. They had been a lean team – a dream team – a dynamic duo even towards the end a Hansel and Gretel who lost the trail of breadcrumbs and couldn't get out of the forest...

She had become lost to him – over inflated by an unknown hand and last seen soaring away into the blue – shot down!

It was on his last case about which...

About which his view – his opinions – his conclusions were still as foggy as this day. Inspector Hedge entered the shop. The place stank of tobacco and the proprietor greeted him with a fag stuck in the corner of his mouth.

'Ello, Inspector 'Edge! I ain't seen you on the rounds for a long time since?

No time for small chat, Arnold my lad. What are you doing with a piece of Met property in your window?

What Met property, mate?

You have an Inflatable Policewoman in your window. Don't deny it.

Oh 'er? Well... That there lady so to speak – to be jocular in manner Inspector – to lift our spirits this damp and overcast day... She – she 'as been decommissioned.

Decommissioned? Who decommissioned her?

Ask me another, Inspector. I don't know who. Come in a job lot, mate, it did. Church bazaar it was.

Was a vicar involved?

I didn't see no vicar – if you will kindly excuse the double negative.

Where was this?

I come by the information second-hand, Inspector. I never went to the church sale.

Inspector Hedge frowned, searching his mind for explanations. It? It? She...? She had been his professional partner. The apparatus was manufactured to give a likeness of the fair sex. Fair enough. No getting away from that. Some might say she was attractive – even lifelike. It was meant to fool the public for a limited time. A drive-past perhaps. A parked lookout. But shortage of police officers – cuts – pushed the inflatables to extend their role and this could mean falling into a personal relationship in the face of danger...

You get my meaning? Hedge said.

Why? What did you say? I can't hear your thoughts, Inspector.

I'll put it this way... when you are out on a case living in such close proximity – out in the cold – only me and her so to speak for days on end even though admittedly she is a manufactured item... But then what do you know? How could a piece of villainy like you understand?

Hedge was getting hot under the collar. Why bother to explain to a toerag? A crafty fence dealing in stolen goods though what was stolen in these parts was hardly worth the effort. He heard himself continuing...

In the economy drive launched by the Yard we were issued with these inflatables – someone's bright idea – to keep the numbers on the street up – a visible presence of the law though I was against the scheme to start with – driving around with a balloon? I soon came to see their uses. It was a piece of equipment that you could personalise to your own tastes. She was the silent type that one. I liked that. No chat. Though she recorded all that was going on oh yes – Doris was a good listener! Or was that the later model? I can't recall. It comes and goes...

He stared at the proprietor the pebble lenses of whose steel rimmed glasses were as filthy as his shop window.

Can you see me through those glasses?

I can 'ear yer, Inspector. And I can 'ear an awful isolation in your heart. How come if I let your Policewoman Doris go to you for a fiver?

With the appropriate paperwork?

I didn't get no paperwork, mate. There ain't no paperwork.

How am I supposed to reopen this case if I don't have the paperwork?

That's your problem, mate. When you step out of that door...

Hedge paid up the five pounds. He was glad to pay – no messing – to have her back – to be reunited with that laughable piece of equipment as some called her! Doris Policewoman 07032 Inflatable, had been forced into retirement from the Force without recourse to appeal. No paperwork. No pension. It could be him next. How shoddy his employers were...

The inspector exited the junk shop with the deflated item in a plastic bag. The fog had thinned a little and he saw a police car approaching. It drew up to the kerb.

Hop in Inspector! We have orders to take you to the Yard. The Super wants to have a little word with you – apparently quite urgent like.

Hedge climbed into the back of the police car. This was more like it.

A policewoman – not of the inflatable variety – was seated beside the driver. As they drove off she turned back with a cheery smile.

Where have you been Jack? Not seen you around recently, have we?

Under-cover, he replied.

In plain wrappers, eh? Guffawed the driver and she joined in.

Inspector Hedge smiled. Keep the party going. Though not to be dignified with any more chat. He always had been regarded as an odd fish at the Yard. Bit of a loner. Not one to join in a conversation. Always had his head stuck in a book. Never mind. You had to suffer fools gladly there...

Was there another case looming?

Is that why he'd been sent for?

Or had they woken up at the Yard and decided not to cave-in to hidden pressures but to reinstate the case which he had not abandoned?

His case...

Don't let it go cold...

He was not about to regardless of why they had called him in. Hedge was ready. The Superintendent wanted to see him and about time too.

2

Hello Hedge! Hello, hello! There's a good chap no need to salute my God we were at Hendon together passing out parade and out on the beat at the same time – a rough apprenticeship eh? Watching out for each other's backs we both made good officer material and you a brilliant detective! Me plodding in admin desk bound – armchair amateur according to some – it's not all about money you know! Pips on your shoulder? No, believe me it's job satisfaction that counts! And you've got bags of that!

Comfy?

Comfy are we?

Like a cup of tea?

Would you?

Biscuit?

Speak up! Don't be shy! My God, it's so good to see you Jack! Yes, though you do look a bit under the weather and we know what the weather's like today. Don't we? Would you like a cup of tea Jack? This is my last offer!

No thank you sir. I appreciate the offer...

The inspector could hear his own voice. Coming in on the conversation. He waited for more. He'd had the overture. Overture for beginners. But he was an old hand. Now for the opera. True, the Super had been a pal – well not too chummy – even in those days. Everyone knew Lenny would get on. Lenny The Lion. And he expected favours as he dished them out. It was the commerce of his job. He expected his inspectors to toe the line – when things went wonky – not exactly a cover-up it was more about protecting the Force from destructive outside influences. But Hedge had no favours to return today.

He was on sick leave, wasn't he? Official...

He was breathing, staying calm waiting – waiting for the axe to fall – for his head to come off – because the moment he walked into the superintendent's office he sensed that something was wrong because the clock was ticking too loudly.

I got the squad car boys to pick you up. They found you. The Super again.

Yes thank you, sir.

Lenny!

Thank you Lenny. Yes, thank you – Lenny...

Well done Jack. Out and about, eh? We all know you're keen but you don't need to be strolling about your old manor in your uniform when you are officially off duty. You know that, I presume?

I know when I am on duty – officially assigned to a case that is – I am Plain Clothes Division yes, explained Hedge. However – how shall I put it?

I'm waiting to hear how you put it.

It's nice to be one of the Boys In Blue again. To be reminded – to remind myself as I might put it – where I belong! Where I've come from... if you get my meaning? Lenny?

Go on. By all means – explain yourself.

I mean it is the uniform I represent in all aspects of my employment. Whether I am wearing it or not. I am the uniform. That's who we are. They love us or hate us for that. It's the uniform does it...

Very well. Point taken. You should not be wearing the uniform when you are on sick leave, Jack. Off duty.

I am never off duty. I'm never not a police officer...

Hedge was sweating. Though the warmth was going out of the meeting. Go on.

I am ready to resume light duties, Lenny. In fact anything Leonard – have a heart – for old time's sake – put me back on the roster – I need to work – I need a case. Don't you see, Lenny, I have never been ill. Not really. I have been drugged on my last job – zombified – got at – interfered with something rotten to get me into the mental hospital – under cover – to investigate an enormous government fudge – disaster – they dare not warn the public...

The Super scratched the slight stubble on his chin, which he thought made him more approachable. Matey.

You believe you were sent on a case?

Into a looney bin?

Jack I know you still have flashbacks. That does not mean there was a case. But even if between these four walls we say there was – we admit there was that possibility of an investigation – it is closed.

You admit there was a case? Hedge said hoarsely.

What I do admit, is that it is difficult for you to tell reality from an hallucination.

But that was my value to you, Lenny. That I was on the cutting edge of reality, where others – the big hitters who think they are out of reach of common law, by the way – with their little deals and rake-offs. None of your other officers could have taken on this case. Who do they think they are? They're playing on the margins of good and evil but I was face to face with it.

You know how that sounds, don't you? Crazy, Jack. Good and evil?

The Superintendent was sitting back in his chair quizzically regarding his inspector. Hedge was breathing heavily.

I tell you sir – Leonard – Lenny – Len – this thing is not finished. It will crop up again in another form. It will not let us go! My God, which side are you on?

The Superintendent was stung. Or played stung.

How dare you? Are you completely mad? Jack? Do you suppose I am in league with the devil, is that it? OK, Inspector Hedge, I have given you enough rope and you have hung yourself. I'll have to be formal with you from now on – pull rank! No alternative...

We have an alternative sir! Come off it – Lenny! Keeping me on sick leave is playing into their hands! Can't you see that?

Hedge was out of the chair pacing the office.

The Super back-pedalled becoming once more indulgent but then he could be mercurial in mood change and it was as if he was always choosing which card to play from his hand. And he made sure he shuffled the pack.

Whose hands exactly are we playing into Jack?

It's our job to find out. Even if it brings the Establishment crashing down round our ears. Something in the state of Denmark is rotten.

Sit down man, please, sit down, said the Super. Or shall I make it an order?

Hedge sat down.

So now we are threatening to bring down the Government, are we? I will have to issue an order. Reluctantly but here it is. Inspector Hedge you are to go home and remove your uniform and you will not wear it again until you are placed back on duty, officially.

Hedge stood up again. Officially? When has my work ever been officially? Not in recent times for sure. I've never been more unofficial. I've been in a nursing home officially as a patient but unofficially under cover and...

YOU PUT ME THERE!

Surprised by his own ferocity Hedge took a deep breath and came back to his chair and sat down and more quietly addressed his boss...

You put me there, Leonard. So why am I still on sick leave? If you regard that case as closed?

The Superintendent stood up and came round the front to assume a more friendly posture perching his posterior on the desk. Go home there's a good boy, will you? Do yourself a favour while there's still time Jack.

I am my uniform...

Hedge was pleading...

Without my uniform I am naked. Even under cover I know my uniform is waiting for me. In my wardrobe. You cannot forbid me to wear it. I've been through the ranks – I've been through hell and high water for that uniform and what it represents. It is who we are – it is what we are – you cannot forbid me to wear my uniform.

That is exactly what I am doing Inspector. You will not make a monkey out of the Met. That uniform is not meant for lunatics to parade around in. I'm sorry – sorry to have to put it like that.

I understand. In that case Lenny, my old friend, you had better have it now, had you not?

Hedge smiled. He took from pockets his badge and wallet and removed his wrist watch. He placed these items upon the Super's desk. Then he took off his uniform jacket and trousers. Shirt and tie followed. The Superintendent followed this display with a wary interest.

Inspector Hedge removed his vest and socks.

Sock suspenders.

Underpants.

He stood naked as a new born babe in front of his boss.

Will that be all, sir?

Yes, I will be referring you for further psychiatric treatment, Inspector Hedge. You may go.

Thank you, sir.

Hedge placed the items he had put on the desk – badge, wallet and wristwatch – into the plastic bag already containing his previous partner, Inflatable Policewoman Doris, 07032. He saluted smartly, turned about and left the office. He strode down the corridor ignoring curious stares from other apparently saner inhabitants of the building. In the lift it was only Policewoman Doris in the plastic bag that hid his manhood from the other passengers. He marched through the vestibule past other people going about their own business with their own concerns.

And out into a world where the fog was lifting.

Upon the white steps of the Yard a shaft of golden sunlight illuminated the nude police inspector in all his glory.

It was a new day.

He was free.

He descended the steps and flagged down a taxi that unflinchingly took the fare. This was London.

Pre-disaster.

Pre-horror.

They drove off.

They drove off into a world as it would become – the hopes and fears of all the years – and the inspector was gone from their dreary routines, their inhibitions and secret hatreds, their loyalties to other than the Good Of The Realm.

3

Fully inflated Policewoman Doris 07302 bobbed up and down in the gentle breeze that wafted in through the open window on a fine spring morning. A blustering Westerly had blown away the smog the week before. Inspector Hedge's flat in Earls Court was spacious and tidy. Lounge, separate bedroom, kitchenette, bathroom and all mod cons. It was in a decent block too. Didn't Anthony Newley have an apartment in the building? That tells you something. Girls in and out all hours. He minded his own business. Behind shut doors who knew what went on, his own closed and bolted front door being a case in point. Though the lust had gone regarding Inflatable Ex-Policewoman Doris now decommissioned. He felt sorry for her if anything. All patched up and nowhere to go. Not much of a life outside of the Force but better with him than residing in a junk shop window. As for himself he was not decommissioned. He had not handed in his badge. Not that stupid. Only his uniform. As a symbolic gesture – like Saint Francis Of Assisi – who had stripped naked in the court of Florence renouncing his father's fortune. And what had he, Inspector Hedge, renounced? Nothing really only the stupidity and gullibility of those in his branch...

Didn't they know what was going on?

Didn't Leonard know?

His Superintendent – the Super – an old pal from Hendon Police College days – not really that pally – but Len knew how to play a game – and what now was he setting Jack Hedge his favourite Detective Inspector up for? Because no one had come round knocking on the door and carted him away to play looney-tunes in a clinic where hidden in a basement were the dying survivors of a government germ warfare experiment that had gone drastically wrong...

It was never that simple. It was easier to ask himself which side was his Super on. But was Lenny ever on any other side except his own? The winning side. Which could of course mean changing sides. It was as if the whole thing had been scripted. But he often felt that. That he was being moved by old traumas he was not aware of. Childhood. The time before memory when terror demanded to be closed down – buried – as if it had never occurred – that awful fear of abandonment placed in a lead-lined box. But the box was leaking, wasn't it? Waves of panic coming from nowhere. Of course he could see a psychiatrist – that bloke he had been referred to – another one in the net of conspiracy to convince him he was mad and to abandon the case. The case in the clinic now closed. A cold case...

The phone rang. Let it ring. If they wanted him they knew where to find him – the most brilliant and unorthodox detective in the department. As it continued ringing after going into the hall and staring at the instrument for some time he picked it up...

Hello, said a voice. It's Shirley. Is that you, Jack?

Her?

Sounding so normal. Hadn't heard from her since their days in the nuthouse together. Shirley, the boy girl boy girl depending what day it was – and her MI5, by her own account. Well she wasn't saying she was Josephine and he wasn't saying he was Napoleon so perhaps they weren't that barmy. They had both survived. Got out alive...

Jack? Are you there?

Hello Shirley. It's been a while.

Yes. By the way the name's Margaret today. That's my real name. Well let's put it this way – that's as real as we're going to get.

Right. I'm still Jack Hedge. And that's as real as I'm going to get.

She laughed. He remembered her laugh. Golden sunshine pouring into the room...

Now we've got that straight, Jack, do you fancy a drink? Like this evening?

OK. Margaret? Margaret, right! Yes, alright. Where did you have in mind?

They met at the Nine Elms, a grotty pub under the viaduct. Popular with pimps, prostitutes, perverts and spies whose offices were local so it was a convenient watering hole. There were also a sprinkling of Maltese criminals around Nine Elms but most of the London low life met in the East End with Your Old Bill to fraternise and decide who could be banged up for a stretch without causing too much bad feeling bearing in mind the families involved. MI5 were different. More likely to be an invisible part of the scenery.

You're famous! She said, laughing and showing a lovely set of white teeth. It's all over the shop! Your strip-off at the Yard, darling! What a hoot! That should convince anyone you're totally off your tree – bonkers! Who put you up to it? She was letting on that she was in the know.

12

Oh you heard, did you? Trust the Met to broadcast that. It must have suited their book, what? He rubbed his forehead. Actually – you see – I was making a point, Margaret.

You don't have to convince me, darling. It was a brilliant move!

If you'd like to know, I feel cleansed by what I did – though naturally they referred me to a psychiatrist because they can't take it, can they?

Obviously not. Let me buy the drinks Jack. I'm on full pay.

So am I for the first six months while the matter is being reviewed. They can review my arse cos I'm not giving up on the case. What case? They say there isn't any case. It's my case that's what and I have yet to bring anyone in.

No-one wants you to give up. No-one expects you to give up. They are providing you with more cover, Jack, my dear. Cover.

Cover? For what? You mean a covert op? I'm a cop plain and simple.

Hang on a mo, she said. Grab that table! She took off to the bar.

He had met her in the nuthouse. She was still playing the same game then? Maybe she was MI5 after all, like she claimed. She had information about him. Well he could string her along and find out...

Hedge got to the only free table before a hairy biker but the intruder plonked himself down in the chair opposite.

That chair's taken mate.

Oh yeah, said the exhibition of body tattoos framed by a leather waistcoat, Who sez?

I sez.

Are you looking for trouble, pretty boy, are you?

I am trouble, said Hedge, producing his badge. Now shove off like a good girl before I find a reason to nick you.

Don't be like that. I was only being friendly.

Margaret came to the table with the drinks. Fuck off, Claude. This is business.

The biker Claude arose and graciously gave up the chair to the woman he obviously knew. He gave Hedge a big smile. Some other time, eh? I can help you get to know yourself better.

Claude fucked off and Margaret sat down.

Are the Russians in tonight? Hedge surveyed the room.

Of course. The more you try and hide things the more important the Reds assume it is. So flaunting this meeting in front of them is more likely to put them off. Cheers!

They drank.

Are we of any interest to the Russians? Asked Hedge.

Absolutely not, darling. But it's for them to find that out. We love wasting their resources.

Inspector Hedge studied the wraith of a girl. On first meeting in the looney bin he had taken her to be a boy and even considered adopting him and opening a private detective agency with him now her well just for today HER.

She smiled brightly, inhaled on the cigarette and let the smoke trickle out of her nose. We might as well dispense with the small talk. We know each other better than to need it. Jack, it's like this...

It hurt Hedge to see her so bright so happy yet ruining her health storing up trouble smoking. Stop. But he said nothing. He never had smoked. He took the occasional beer. He was a health fanatic and determined to live as near forever as was possible these days...

It's like this. There is no case on record. So you could not have been booted off a case that did not exist. You were sick in a psychiatric clinic and dreamt the whole episode up. Isn't that nice? Of a government germ warfare experiment that went disastrously wrong and you were sent to the nursing home which housed the victims, dying off. All that was the product of your fevered unbalanced mind, darling, right?

Very convenient, muttered Hedge.

The only case on the record, darling – is your medical record.

Hedge sniffed and squeezed his eyes to be rid of the smoke haze that infiltrated every corner of the bar. What about off the record? Isn't that why you phoned to meet me in this den of iniquity?

Off the record, darling...

She leant forward grasping his arm. Off the record I want you to keep believing in your sanity. That you haven't made anything up. To at least keep an open mind on that possibility. Is that too difficult for you?

I'm used to asking the questions. Let me remind you. I met you in the clinic. So what were you doing there? Never mind me. Were you sick? Or playing sick? MI5? Were you? Are you? How the hell do I know? You were just another crazy bird locked up to save you from self-harming, as far as I was concerned.

She stubbed out the cigarette. It sizzled in the wet ashtray. She gave the noise space before answering. Of course I was playing the game. It was set up that I go into the clinic and support you. We were both so fucked up on their drugs, darling, it was difficult to focus on our mission. Or was I another patient? Simply part of your fantasising? Joining in until the doctors twigged it and separated us? For our own good of course. And do I still want to play? Isn't spying called The Big Game, Jack?

Margaret – if that's your latest name – listen – you told me – you just told me when we met – you said they are providing me with more cover. For what?

To go deeper.

Deeper? What? Where?

They're not sure. But they want you out in the field – a loose cannon – apparently off sick. And you played into that beautifully with your exciting striptease in the Superintendent's office. Was it agreed between you, was it?

Between who?

You and Lenny?

Lenny? Oh we're on first name terms with my Superintendent now, are we? Very cosy. I didn't agree anything. My striptease, so called, was made on a matter of principle. I am my uniform!

She moved to grip his hand now. Tight. We've both been fucked up, Jack. For the Cause. It had to be like that to give the covert op any chance of succeeding. And it's not over, believe me. There have been meetings and this is one of them. They are not – I repeat not – deactivating you.

I could deactivate myself.

No. You won't do that. I know you...

She got very confidential.

Believe me, there is a case. Call it if you like, yes, 'code name green swan' – where did you get that from?

The bottom of the lake...

Maybe your naked gesture wasn't sick. But you're not going to start a monastic order, are you? Let's say that it was a brilliant ploy set up by you and the Super. Everyone is convinced you're mad. You have deep cover.

Thanks.

She stood up, gazing down at him all sweetness and light.

Must rush, sweetie. Keep the faith! We'll be in touch...

And she was gone, vanishing through the crowded hubbub of the saloon bar and the loud chatter that buzzed and clanged as words collided and shattered and fell at random into deaf ears. Margaret not Shirley – give her a name – had left a phone number on a slip of paper. Was that it? Was that all? A reassurance that he was still on the job? He was inclined to believe her. He wanted to believe her – he wanted to identify himself with – with something. He had to be careful, it was his Achilles heel, his feeling that he wasn't real. It came and went.

Focus, she said. Yes, focus...

Was she the ex-patient he had met in the puzzle factory and still playing a fantastical game?

Or was she indeed MI5? He decided, as if it mattered, that she was MI6 now.

More to the point was he convalescing after a psychotic spell in hospital? After being sectioned into a clinic buried in the heart of the countryside where he had dreamt up and lived in every fibre of his being, a case he labelled *Code Name Green Swan?* Or had it actually, in your face, happened? To him and to the country he still believed in and served. This Emerald Isle set in a silver sea in dire peril of a return of the Great Plague last experienced in 1665 in London. And what did that consignment of tinned corned beef really contain? Time to go...

Leaving an unfinished pint of bitter on the table Inspector Hedge pushed through the mix of mental defectives seeking salvation in each other's sweat and spit and left the pub. He walked over Vauxhall Bridge and along the Embankment. A fine night. That's what he enjoyed doing – walking – a bobby on the beat! That was the best part of the job, all weathers, him. He hadn't wanted to skulk away in a patrol car devouring hamburgers and getting an enlarged waist-line. Nor had he looked forward to promotion to a desk job. Detective work he had aimed at and that's what he was – a detective. Deep breaths. Yes, a lovely evening. He would soon be back home with Ex-Policewoman Doris. He didn't like to leave her too long on her own. Not after what she had been through – over-inflated and shot down out of the sky abandoned and lost in the brutal goings on during Code Name Green Swan. He was waiting to get a handle on it. That's what his Granny used to say, I'll wait until life tells me. Life would tell him too. He cut through Pimlico and passed over one of the railway bridges down from Victoria Station. By the time he had walked to Sloane Square it had started to rain. A drizzle. Good. Down the Kings Road quiet now then turn north up to Earls Court. The key was in the door and he was unlocking it. Yes life would tell him. Thanks Granny

4

He had received a letter instructing him to visit a certain Doctor Fettle the following Tuesday morning at 11am at an address in Harley Street. He was to bring along all the medications that he was taking. That was a laugh! The meds had gone into the Thames care of the sewers and would be changing the sex lives of the fishes. He had no intention of going to Harley Street for a consultation – not after what he knew about Doctor Fettle – or suspected he knew – or imagined he knew. What did he know? He had been treated by Doctor Fettle while he was in the clinic and he had no intention of falling into his prescriptive clutches again. The medical facility had been aiding and abetting a government germ warfare experiment that had gone badly wrong – people had died. It was Top Secret. It had never happened. There was no *Code Name Green Swan* that left them with a nutty policeman to suspend from duties and dispose of as and when.

Inflatable Policewoman Doris was still there, bobbing gently up and down on the settee. She had been in the thick of things with him. She was patched up from bullet holes and wore an expressionless face that hid the horror of her witness of events in the unresolved case. She had been junked! Discovered in a second-hand furniture shop in Shepherds Bush. I know, Doris, he said, that you are an extension of my imagination as far as company is concerned – sociability – all that stuff – that stuff that people do – that he had done and failed at so dismally – that not to fail so painfully he had withdrawn from intimate relationships and truth to tell nobody bothered him either. He had been married once but she had left him after pronouncing him to be very boring. She, Alice, wanted excitement and she had found it in the bottle, so he was well rid of her though he had heard... had heard... not for a long time now. He, Jack, had his own traumas – the boy who had been so reluctant to throw out his teddy bear but he had done it under duress from his father: son, you are getting bullied because you take a teddy bear to school and you are thirteen years old when are you going to grow up? So he had binned his teddy.

And written a story...

Teddy had escaped from the dustbin and fallen in with some other cast-out soft toys and dolls all in a state of dishevelment button eyes hanging loose torn limbs leaked stuffing a squeak moved to a foot. They had formed a band and they lived in a squat under the tyrannous tutelage of a punk doll whose golden locks has been sheared off by a child experimenting with hair styles who had then panicked and thrown her toy into the river and told her mother it had been stolen by a gang of nasty boys...

Now he was a police inspector. Hard working, respected for his diligence, perseverance and case-cracking talents and equally hated for these qualities by idle bobbies that found this threatening. He had no time to write children's stories, not while he was in a state of suspension, perhaps one day when he retired. Which he was not about to do in the face of a monstrous deceit. Meanwhile, the Clean Air Act was being promulgated in Parliament and the sun got to hear of it and came out to play. He did not go and see Doctor Fettle and ignored follow-up letters giving him new appointments.

One day he deflated Doris and put her back in the plastic bag – nothing personal – and he thought about Alice his ex a lot. At the beginning it had been such fun. Though he had not been able to keep up with Alice's partying which went on with or without actual parties. She was very glad of someone to pick up the pieces and he felt significant in the role of minder. He was looking after her. He was her husband which rounded off his sense of identity. Even though she phoned him at work to come and get her out of scrapes or could he join her in an afternoon drinking club which did annoy him but it was the wife wasn't it? The wife, yes, which added texture to his life. It's your wife again Jack, can you pick-up on line six? She needed him, didn't she? Someone in the world valued him. Or devalued him but he could take it the rough with the smooth and yes she did she did need him. Which was why it was all the more surprising when she left him one fine day or was it raining for an army bod a major somebody hyphen hyphen to help spend his inheritance and retirement annuity. He had let Alice divorce him and go to the devil in Brighton and Hove with her Major Fortesque hyphen hyphen whatever he called himself MC and bar though. She may have married her Major or not but they had had a bust up – then got back together so she – Alice – was not knocking on his door asking to be forgiven was she? And he was still better off on his own and last he heard the Galloping Major who rode horse to hunt and had died last he heard. Were they back from Rhodesia? Or did she bring the body home more like? Her in widow's weeds and gin-soaked to lay his mortal remains to rest in the family seat with lots of tears and now what's left of that inheritance? She had come into some money which she would know how to get through like a dose of salts the Merry Widow! He could see it all, picture the scene, he pictured too many scenes. He had lost touch with Alice...

Doctor Fettle had phoned his home number. Quite friendly. Professional. Advising him to come in, please, just for a chat and we'll take it from there just let me know when you're coming in Inspector Hedge because while you don't keep in touch and probably don't take your meds there is a real chance that you will suffer another episode. Thanks. I'll think about it. Phone down. Quite abrupt. What?

WHAT BLOODY EPISODE?

Was he in a Police series now, was that it? Episode One, we'd had that. Very dangerous too it had been for the health of Yours Truly. Episode One – *THE INCURABLES* – *The Case Of The Green Swan*. He was the star of the drama and it had gone so well there was now another episode in the offing that's what the doctor had said. Doctor Fettle. If he did not take his medication he would have another episode. Well he was up for it bring it on lad, his own crime series. Of course there would be another bloody episode. Because nothing had been resolved the miscreants had not been put away, had they? And the viewers were mystified. The public had a right to know. Their appetite was whetted they wanted more. And he was ready, *Another Inspector Hedge Case*. Right! Got it! After which nothing happened hours turning into days into weeks and in the moment of it all he lost heart. He considered the possibility yes perhaps he was psychotic. It was only the fact that he had met Margaret who maybe was as deluded as he was but then again they could both be sane. On the case. Which would be inviting a response from some dangerous people out there and you could include Doctor Fettle in that lot...

Ha ha, he had an episodic illness so he had a lot to look forward to as did all his listeners or viewers or readers. His illness could arrange itself into a series of episodes. Series One...

Inspector Hedge – the almost real Inspector Hedge by his own reckoning – kept a low profile only going out at night and making sure he was not being tailed. At any time he expected a knock on the door and a paper waved under his nose – official notification that his civil rights had been rescinded as it had been decided that he was a danger to himself and others – before they forcibly restrained him and took him away in an ambulance. This is like Russia he decided, when Stalin was alive and they knocked on doors in the early hours or lifted people off the streets. Artists musicians composers and three star generals. Even writers of children's stories. He had the slip of paper in his wallet with her phone number. Margaret. Him her him her take your pick. Currently her. He read a lot. Reading books. Serious literature did not go down well at the Yard like when he attempted to discuss Albert Camus and existentialism in the Police canteen. That had been the start of his unpopularity and the nodding and laughing behind his back...

But there was no knocking on his door or ringing on the bell at 5am. Instead one morning an envelope was thrust through his letter-box. It contained travel documents to Berlin and a passport giving him an assumed identity as Mr Green, a travelling salesman in iron ore. He was booked into the Hotel Hermann on the Behrenstrabe and was to wait there until someone contacted him. Someone wanted him in Berlin? Assume his employers. Assume nothing...

5

Berlin was a huge building site. Jackhammers noisily pounded pilings into foundations. Cement was poured endlessly into mounds of wire mesh and buildings grew as cranes filled the skyline moving about nodding like a colony of wild geese during the mating season. At Tempelhof Airport Herr Hess waited at Arrivals for the passengers to emerge from BA Flight 1052 from London, Heathrow, which had just landed. It was a hot afternoon in Berlin and Hess was sweating. Nothing new in that. He was known to sweat even in winter. He had sweated a lot during his trial for war crimes but had escaped the rope and got off relatively lightly considering. Considering the people he had killed. But he was only obeying orders. He was still obeying orders. And still killing people. As the passengers began to exit Herr Hess held up a piece of cardboard, written upon it MR GREEN. But the aforesaid Mr Green had cashed in his ticket in London and bought another flight that happened to be available and Mr Green was now arriving at Keflavik International Airport, Reykjavik, in Iceland,

From Hedge's hotel window he could catch sight of the impressive Hallgrimskirkja Church tower. That could be said of most hotel windows in Reykjavik, given that they were facing in the right direction. He methodically unpacked items from the suitcase, placing them in drawers and hanging garments in the wardrobe. He stowed the suitcase in the wardrobe. He had not deflated Policewoman Doris and brought her. No he had left his fantasies behind. Though there was still a problem which was what was fact and what was a drug-imposed hallucination he had suffered on the last case?

He could sort it....

Hedge lay upon the the Queen-size bed and considered his options. He felt reasonably sure that they had decided to delete him, surplus to requirements, he was in fact not a fantasy a danger to the Establishment given all he knew. It was logical and what better way to dispose of him than to lose him on a mission. That was it. Easier than having to fake an accident and dispose of a body in Earls Court, Berlin was a better bet. Still raw and new divided by the Four Powers with the Cold War going on. He knew they would come after him sooner or later though he did not know who they were. Rather than let them choose the killing field he had cashed in the one-way ticket to Berlin. Reykjavik was as good a choice as any. Of course they would come after him but they would be disconcerted. Disorganised. It was no longer neat – arranged – all paid for and no trails leading back to head office. But which head office?

There were a lot of head offices in London, some with their own headed writing paper and others more obscure. You could go up in the lift or down to the sewers, it depended on the service you were working for.

Or who was serving who?

Were the politicians any longer in charge of the monsters they had created?

For example a germ warfare experiment had gone badly wrong – not only had all the infected scientists kicked the bucket or been kicked into the bucket but the public could still be in danger. They wanted to take back control – them – to deal with things on their terms – to keep the dissemination of information or disinformation in their own hands. They did not want to be shown up as bloody fools, as negligent, as responsible. It came naturally. The Defence Of The Realm they called it.

A Realm that could be about to be overwhelmed by a return of The Black Plague. Of course, that would have some beneficial effects like giving the economy a much needed boost as had the Great Plague some centuries before. Labour had become in very short supply, wages had shot up, more housing was freed up – unintentional effects but the Government would be working on a Plan B. A State Of Emergency was always a good idea, a self-serving and convenient way to curtail democratic rights. If a third of the population died quickly, well afterwards the NHS would find things a lot easier...

There was a discreet tap upon his door. Discretion is the better part of valour. Hedge was unarmed. They could not have got to him already, surely? The person – or several people – whoever it was – whoever they were – had not come through reception. They had turned up outside his door unannounced. It could be room service. The door was unlocked. Careless of him but an assassin would have been in the room by now. Job done! Hedge stood up from the bed and called out,

Enter!

A cheerful mop of blond curls poked into the room.

Hello, Mr Green!

Blondie entered the room and it was filled with a large Nordic presence… a ham hand was extended.

Gisli! Gisli Johansen! I am so glad to make your acquaintance!

Hedge did not attempt to shake the hand on offer. He was ready to smash the fellow with a chair if he attempted a wrong move. Behind a radiant smile the man was talking. Forgive my butting in, my dear chap, were you resting? Sleeping perhaps? It's hard to tell night from day here at this time of year it never gets dark – a few hours of gloaming when possibly a minor crime or two might take place but relatively speaking – and everything is relative as Albert Einstein observed – Reykjavik is a safe city I assure you! Until it isn't which of course can be any time. Meanwhile you can go about your business with impunity! The man paused. He looked round the room. Do tell me, sir, are you quite comfortable in your room?

Inspector Hedge considered how he should answer this already familiar person. Yes, there is a view of the cathedral.

Good. We will of course be picking up the tab.

Hedge stared blankly at the intruder. I was not expecting a reception committee.

One step ahead of the game, Mr Green! It is the only way to win! It is the only game in town! Gisli sat down on the settee and lounged comfortably back his long legs stretched out. Mr Green, I have come a long way and night being day and day being night one never gets accustomed to it at this time of year though I have been born with it. I hope you don't mind if I have a power nap. He yawned and dropped off to sleep.

Leaving the Icelandic intruder to his dreams the inspector stepped into the hotel corridor shutting the door quietly behind him. He took the lift up to the roof café where the view of the cathedral was even better, found a table and ordered 'Kaffi og Kaka' otherwise known as coffee and cake. Delicious. The café was busy, the Icelanders are known to have a very sweet tooth and lots of excellent dentists.

Hedge pondered. It seemed like the good guys knew he was coming so somebody was on his side. Perhaps he could have gone to Berlin as directed and not taken evasive action. But someone had alerted the appropriate Reykjavik department and they had quickly got on the job. He – Jack Hedge – did not know what the job was and it was possible that no-one else did either. Paper shuffling department to department could lead to random decisions long after a master plan had disintegrated. It was a matter of continual activity and justifying your job. Well he had made his own decision random enough so play along for now...

Some twenty minutes later a dishevelled Gisli joined him, slumping down onto the chair opposite. I was out of it man! I am restored to full power after that little nap! Like your famous Winston Churchill who liked power naps – it helped him win the war! I feel so much power that I could be plugged in to the National Grid but with our many waterfalls providing hydro electric energy plus the thermal waters which provide heating I am not needed so I will save my energy for other things! Like your protection, Mr Green. Gisli Johansen ordered a beer, took a deep swig, wiped the froth from his lips and beamed across the table. My dear Mr Green! How are you enjoying your holiday?

I am not your dear Mr Green, replied Hedge. Let's get one thing straight. I am the wrong Mr Green neither dear nor otherwise I have come here on a private holiday with no meetings planned.

That is excellent news! It is the wrong Mr Green I have been waiting for. Not the right Mr Green. I missed you at the airport. By a whisker! All the right Mr Greens are not in Reykjavik believe me. Some are in Golders Green in London. I don't know where the others are. You are definitely the wrong Mr Green – you said it your self – so there is no mistake! Please do not worry about it. Would you like another beer?

I have not had the first beer. I don't drink.

OK. Very good, Mr Green. Do you know the north of Iceland? Its high mountains deep valleys – its lava fields and mud baths – its bays in which whales abound! All are of great interest! Ice! Light! Reflection! Would you like to visit these areas?

Hedge stared out of the panoramic window. The iconic cathedral tower was having a hypnotic effect.

Would you very much like the trip, Mr Green? Possibly? Probably? Mathematically? Gisli frowned comically. Such matters can be calculated. It is the basis of statistics upon which life insurance premiums are based. I should know because I was an insurance agent once upon a time – not a government agent. But this is of no interest to you. I can calculate your life expectancy. Mathematically. I do it automatically. So that the company never loses. He laughed. That is the important thing. The company must not lose. Nor must other interests lose today in the situation in which we are placed. We could go to the Blue Lagoon with its hot and healing waters, yah? Rich in silicone it refreshes and smooths the skin like a babies bottom! Would you like to go there, Mr Green? While you are in Iceland? On your holiday? You have hired me to be your guide.

Have I?

I must tell you that you are not behaving like a typical tourist. Please show some interest. Help me do my job, eh? Do call me Gisli, I am at your service, sir.

I did not ask hotel reception for a tourist guide. You arrived outside my room touting for business.

You know why I am here, the Icelander winked. Listen. Listen. He was nodding. My brother died recently in a car crash. I still see him from time to time. He told me it is good to die young so...? He shrugged and smiled edged in pain. So no worries, eh? Gisli stood up. Let us visit the Hallgrimskirkja Church. It is a work in progress – it is unfinished – like all of us, eh? I am a work in progress – you are a work in progress – what part do we have in our own construction? Or deconstruction? These are philosophical questions. Which we might get round to. I would value your take on it...

They were in the Hallgrimskirkja Church. It was a great work in progress as was the drama that Inspector Hedge fully expected would soon enfold him. He looked round the high vaults of the unfinished church in wonder. When do they install the organ? He asked.

Soon, replied Gisli, it is going to be a fantastic organ. Well soon in terms of history it will be completed. But more must be added to the fabric of the church first. That is obvious. The acoustics will be most original. Come back in ten years – twenty years, who knows? Can I call you by your Christian name, by the way?

Jack.

OK, Jack. Here is the gist of it....

Gisli looked round to make sure no-one was close and as that was the case said in a lower register, We leave for Bergen tonight. It will be by trawler – anonymously – and we hope for a fair crossing to Norway. The weather looks good, are you a good sailor?

I don't know, I've never tried.

A couple of tourists passed nearby. The woman had a camera. Gisli spoke in a louder voice. It is said that the church organ when it arrives though only a dream at present is to be installed with over five thousand pipes. Think of that? Think big! We always do, Icelanders! We are a small population in Iceland but rate education and literacy as vitally important.

Can you get me a gun? asked Hedge.

Did you have something in mind? Our minds are peculiar places, are they not? It is said by some philosophers that everything starts there – in the mind – including all of Creation. This makes us very privileged.

A Walther PPK would do nicely.

An excellent choice. Ammunition is readily available for that make. Gisli stood up. Do you want to say a prayer before we go? I will wait at the entrance. He left the pew and walked down the aisle. Hedge watched him go – loose limbed easy aware – an animal. An animal who dozed off like a cat in a power nap and one that could wake up in an instant and pounce.

Hedge knelt as if in prayer. It was important to look normal but was it normal to pray in Reykjavik?

6

Back at the hotel Inspector Hedge sat upon his bed and pondered, was his life being taken over by the enigmatic Mr Green? The wrong Mr Green? His assumed identity? But was not all identity assumed? Inspector Hedge had enough trouble assuming his own identity. Which was one of the reasons – let's face it – why he had joined the police force. The uniform! Which he had so dramatically shed in protest at being ordered not to wear it while on sick leave. Not wise to revisit that. He sometimes thought that there was no such thing as identity – it was a moving landscape that one inhabited and no sooner claimed than it was liable to be snatched from you. Take being a husband – no don't take being a husband it was too painful – one day he was and the next he was a pitiful divorcee – for she who needed him so much that at times he had humorously regarded himself as a minder for this eccentric and beautiful butterfly who could not cope with the daily rituals of life or who could not be bothered – that she Alice had abandoned him and gone off with another bloke? His whole identity as being a needed minder come what may had been shredded. Was that the start of his nervous breakdown?

A breakdown he had been invited to adopt. To get into the clinic. That was then and this was now. Now he had been invited to assume the role of the wrong Mr Green – and where would that lead? To a feeling of panic. Deep breaths. He would not inflate Policewoman Doris. That would be too easy. This was not the time. Concentrate. She – no not the inflatable she – what did she want? Who was she? Was there another half of himself out there somewhere – his better half – waiting to be joined up to him or were they destined to be two halves who could never get together?...

But Margaret?

What about her?

Was she MI5?

Now there was a case of shifting identities and he was still not sure who she was. Margaret was a landscape that changed according to the weather or according to an Ice Age or the raising of sea levels that had swamped the land-link of Britain to the continent of Europe. She was...

Changeable.

Inspector Hedge examined his face in the mirror. Was that the person he had been talking to? Or thinking about? The trouble was – the trouble was he had been injected – doped up something rotten on his last case and was still prone to the odd hallucination. Which was what they – they – they loved the idea of confusing him about reality – them – the bastards! They had set him up and he was not finished with them. He was tenacious. It was a character trait and such a trait could be a clue to identity despite all the bloody changes going on. He cleaned his teeth with bicarbonate to keep the tea stains at bay. He sighed. He – him – endless thought. Awareness? Was that the route to wisdom? He would play along with the wrong Mr Green while bearing in mind that he was Inspector Hedge. Jack Hedge. Divorced. That's who he was...

While Inspector Hedge was considering his options at the same time arriving at Reykjavik Keflavik Airport was a flight from Berlin. Amongst the passengers was Herr Albert Hess. What was his state of mind? Phlegmatic. He went where his orders took him and did what he was told. He was a good boy, his mother had told him that often, patting his head. He had risen rapidly in the Hitler Youth. But that's enough of Herr Hess! Let him remain an enigmatic figure. Suffice to say he lacked a moral compass, enjoyed a laugh and took pleasure in inflicting violence upon his fellow man. Peace was not his thing. He thanked *Gott* for the Cold War which had rescued him from the scrap heap. He sent postcards to his white-haired mother in the care home and she was glad to hear from her only child.

Meanwhile his mother waited with confidence – as did the other residents – for the return of Adolph Hitler. From Bolivia? Or was the Fuhrer plotting his return from elsewhere? An underground cavern somewhere? Where with his brilliant scientists were developing new miracle weapons that would subdue the Allies?

Coming from customs into the arrivals hall Herr Hess proceeded to the toilet and entered a cubicle. He was followed by a man who entered the adjoining cubicle. A Beretta M951 was slid under the partition. Hess placed the pistol into an empty shoulder holster. He also took possession of a spare ammunition clip. Thus was Herr Hess weaponised. He flushed the toilet and exited the cubicle. He washed his hands thoroughly, dried them and left the toilet. A few moments later Gisli Johansen exited the adjoining cubicle vacated the toilet and hurried back to the car park. Why being paid as one man was he called upon to do the job of two? But he needed the money, no use complaining...

Johansen picked up Inspector Hedge outside the hotel at about midnight though it was hardly what you would call dark. The Skoda 1.1 litre Felicia convertible was indeed as its name suggested, a happy car. One you could whistle a happy song in as the wind played in your hair. The car had arrived open to the sky but the Icelander who did not apparently feel the cold had solicitously suggested that he could put the hood up if his passenger would like?

No, no, not necessary...

They were driving north towards the The Port of Isafjordur. An hour out of Reykjavik the inspector changed his mind so they stopped in a lay-by while Gisli fixed the car roof. They climbed back into the Skoda. While we're about it, said Gisli, I will give you the pistol you ordered. No charge, of course, all part of the service, sir! And no questions asked. He took a Walther PPK from the glove compartment, sleek well oiled and loaded and handed the weapon to Hedge. He checked the sleek revolver, found it to be satisfactory and put it away.

They were soon on their way again. This car can do 70 miles an hour, explained Gisli. But I have souped it up to 90 miles an hour – not bad eh, Mr Green? Maybe we are not on Christian name terms? I will not presume. You can call me Gisli – or Hey You Bastard Where Do You Think You're Going? He laughed. Listen, Mr Green! Jack? No, Mr Green – The Wrong Mr Green! Listen, we have a five hour drive ahead of us to get to Isafjordur so maybe we can become pals, eh? How about it? You could tell me about your love life it would keep me awake.

It didn't keep me awake, said Hedge.

Hey, that is funny, yah? Yah, I think so, very funny! Gisli laughed until he had laughed enough and then he stopped laughing. Would you like the heater on?

No thanks.

OK. Gisli whistled tunelessly then renewed his conversation. It will be getting light soon. When we drive through Westfjords you can admire the fantastic scenery. It is most striking. Mountains and lakes! Fiords! Nature reserves! Bird sanctuaries! Tell me, Mr Green, are you circumcised?

No. I am not. I don't have to demonstrate that to you. I am an uncircumcised Mr Green, I never pretended otherwise so if you want to abort this mission let's turn round and go back to Reykjavik and you can wait for a Mr Green who is circumcised. Never mind the scenery.

I did not mean to upset you.

I made very clear at the outset that I am the wrong Mr Green.

Johansen shrugged his wide shoulders. Beggars cannot be choosers.

Look we could stop off somewhere and have a swim. Would you like that?

I don't have a costume.

Wild swimming! Naked!

So that you can see whether I'm circumcised?

No, I take your word for it. Look here. As far as I am concerned any Mr Green will do. I am the delivery boy – I am delivering a Mr Green. If they are complaining because you are not circumcised they can take it up with you! I tell you beyond a certain point I do not care – you are one more delivery and that's it.

Why is it important to you whether I am Jewish or not?

It is important to you, Mr Green, not to me. In fact it is pivotal to your mission. Let me explain, it will pass the time. Norway produces heavy water and Israel needs heavy water to produce the atom bomb which they swear they do not have and do not want. And because, Mr Green, just as important for Israel is to stop Egypt producing the atom bomb which means stopping them obtaining heavy water from Norway. For the same reasons, get it? I wondered which side of the fence you are on, mate?

Hedge was silent, staring out of the window at the scenery which had become as fabulous as predicted – mountains lakes and fiords melting into each other in the morning mist. At last he spoke,

You seem to know a lot about why I'm going to Norway?

It is conjecture, Mr Green. All conjecture. Let's say that you are purchasing heavy water? For someone? And someone else will be trying to stop you. That is clear eh? You see I have a degree in economics so it's pretty easy to work that out. It's like this, I am protecting you and the good die young, like my brother, you remember? Who I saw recently. In the hotel bar. He was across the bar – he smiled – then he was gone.

Hedge said, Yes. It was probably an hallucination.

You are the hallucination, Mr Green. My brother loves me. If you are the wrong Mr Green that could be dangerous.

And if I was the right Mr Green?

Yes, well – that could be dangerous too. You have to decide. I would like to know where the attack is coming from? Johansen's attention returned to the road and the task of manoeuvring its torturous bends. Fortunately it was deserted of traffic coming the other way. The Skoda Felicia was chugging up a mountain pass. The pasty half light was giving way to the dawn and Inspector Hedge could make out the magnificent ravines that plunged down one side of the road, the sheer rock face climbing on the opposite side of the road up away from them obscuring the sky... An eagle soared out of the chasm and he remembered his dreams of flying. What sort of Mr Green was he supposed to be? The passport said British. It was a fake identity but today it felt more real than being Inspector Hedge. It was a long way home...

When he woke up the car was descending rapidly. What was wrong with the brakes? Johansen was whistling. He liked to live dangerously. It was obviously a more intense experience he was seeking. The light – daylight – more light was flooding off an expanse of water. They were descending to a fiord...

Good morning, Mr Green! Shouted Gisli above the creaking machinery of the vehicle. If we survive the descent we will have arrived. It is a half decent motel, OK for a toilet break and for breakfast!

Good, said Hedge, hanging on to the car door.

And to have a ciggy! With one hand only on the wheel Gisli was taking out a packet of cigarettes.

Never smoked! Don't intend to start now!

Mercifully the road levelled out running along the water's edge. By the roadside daffodils danced. And the words danced with them as he recited out loud,

Beside the lake, beneath the trees, fluttering and dancing in the breeze...

The impossible daffodils so far north – so fragile – so brave...

Continuous as the stars that shine and stretch along the Milky Way,
They stretch in never-ending line, Along the margin of the bay
ten thousand saw I at a glance, tossing their heads in sprightly dance...

He was the pooftah police constable who once upon a time carried round a book of poetry and on the night beat stood under street lamps committing verses to memory. Those days were gone. Brave days. Brave as the yellow daffodils dancing as the poet Wordsworth had predicted...

Johansen skidded the Skoda into the forecourt of the motel, braked to a halt and turned off the engine. He sat there a moment his giant hands resting on the steering wheel. He announced, I am sorry to say I have a bad feeling about this job. He turned to look at his passenger. His delivery. And I am seldom wrong, Mr Green. Can you help me out? What's your take on this? Inspector Hedge answered,

And oft when on my couch I lie, In vacant or in pensive mood
They flash upon the inward eye, Which is the bliss of solitude,
Johansen joined in,
And then my heart with pleasure fills, And dances with the daffodils.

The Nordic Prince of the morning exploded with laughter. Beautiful! William Wordsworth! Your Lakeland poet! Here is an Icelandic poem for you:

Coffee and cake, Coffee and cake,
The witches are coming, the witches bake!
Coffee and cake, Coffee and cake,
The witches are coming, to make or to break!
Coffee and cake, Coffee and cake,
To prayers young and old, this day for Christ's sake...

Who wrote that? Asked Hedge.

Anonymous. Come. Breakfast. And I'm bursting for a piss!

They alighted the car – stretching stiff limbs – breathing the invigorating air in magical draughts. The two men entered the motel...

7

Mutti? Are you there, Mutti? Can you hear me?

I am not deaf Albert. Where are you? Why are you phoning me?

I am in Iceland, Mutti. On a job. Your son is in Iceland.

Iceland? Is Adolph Hitler there?

Of course not. Stop with your obsession about Adolph Hitler, Mutti. Hitler is dead. He is not in Iceland.

He is not on ice? He is not refrigerated? The Fuhrer?

No, he is an ex-Fuhrer now. An extinct Fuhrer. Every time I tell you you forget. Adolph Hitler died in the ruins of the Reichstag in 1945. How many more times must I repeat this news?

What news, Albert? When are you coming to see me, Albert? Always on a Thursday. Donnerstag, Albert! Donnersstag!

Not this Donnerstag, Mutti. I must go now...

Coffee and cake, Coffee and cake,

The witches are coming, to make or to break...

Coffee and cake, Coffee and cake,

To prayers young and old, for our Saviour's sake...

8

At the breakfast counter Inspector Hedge avoided choosing one of the large iced buns, the famous Snudur bun, the secret food that kept Icelanders high during long dark winter nights. These were days full of light and anyway he did not need a prolonged sugar buzz. Instead he had chosen hafragrautur, a hot dish of oatmeal porridge mixed with blueberries. Though light streamed through the windows it was still early morning and Jack sat alone in the dining room drinking strong black coffee. Johansen had gone to make a phone call in the foyer and probably to smoke a beloved ciggy. Hedge pondered. Was it after all conceivable that he was the right Mr Green?

Not the wrong Mr Green?

Had they – whoever they were – cottoned on that quickly? Realising that he had done a runner to Iceland? And improvised a reception committee in the shape of Gisli Johansen?

Our Man in Reykjavik?

And adapted for him – the stalwart Inspector – a new identity with a new narrative?

A new Mr Green to serve an Icelandic story that would thrust him forward into an uncertain future?

Did they – whoever the hell they were – have various narratives in different countries and cities waiting to be used? A sort of bespoke mission – would you like to try this story on for size sir – a bit tight round the waist but we can let it out and take the trousers up. Do you dress right or left, sir?

Johansen returned from the foyer. He threw himself into the chair opposite, stretching his long legs out. It's a shit-storm! A fucking shit-storm! It's all starting to unravel my God. Don't think this is the end. We have reached the beginning of Act Three, my friend! The bloody drama! With both hands he massaged his scalp shaking his blond curls out. He gazed quizzically upon the inspector. You are my package. All I want to do, Mr Green, is to deliver you and get the fuck back to Reykjavik. So you're a nice guy? What's that to do with anything? Anything at all? You love poetry, so what? I love poetry. We are not here to start a fucking Poets Society! We have the lakes in Iceland you have the Lakeland poets in England. Wordsworth, Keats, Shelley, Mary Shelley, Lord Byron! Who is fucking who? Who is fucking who on this job? They gave me two jobs today it was a busy day! I was grateful I need the money – fuck I've got two wives three kids – and I live on my own. You tell me? We are pals now! I cannot help wondering if the two jobs are related – there was such a damn rush to get me to the Airport to make a delivery and then back to town to find you. I had to weaponise an incoming visitor. Are the two jobs related today? Who is saving money getting me to do both of them? Look out! But you do not blab in my business. Just because you are a nice fellow does not mean I should be warning you. Tell me Mr Green – sincerely – do you have any reason to believe that you are being followed?

I have a thousand reasons. Reason number one is my paranoia.

But you were not followed from England?

How would I know?

Or from Berlin?

So that was it. Alarm bells were ringing for Hedge. Had the Berlin contact been redirected so quickly? Had they – Yes They – And They Knew Who They Were – had they been thrown into such a panic by his switching flights that they had needed to use Johansen on two jobs? In contradiction to each other?

The Icelander was inviting him to join the dots. The Blonde Bombshell had gone to the airport to meet someone arriving from Berlin and to weaponise them. He only had his word for this story...

Hedge said, I would say we'd be lucky to have any idea who we're working for. Since you asked.

Johansen smiled his broad beaming smile. Did I ask you? Mr Green? I did not realise. It is not my business. I don't the hell know who I work for. Not interested. Not healthy to be interested. Listen I used to play hockey good – ice hockey what else – professional until I bust my spine up anyway – all fixed but end of that career, mate. All I know is that this outfit pay me good. Perhaps you know, Mr Green who is my paymaster? Perhaps you? Because I the fuck don't. I talk too much. This is what I have to tell you. Listen, I made the call. As instructed. We cannot proceed. The trawler has suffered an engine fault. It is in harbour being repaired and it will take an estimated twelve to eighteen hours. We are to wait here until further instructions. This makes us vulnerable Mr Green on your lovely little holiday – does it not – you get that? For which reason obviously you required a Walther PPK? Because you collect World War Two guns? It is your hobby?

What about belt buckles? Cap badges? This job stinks...

Gisli yawned. Fucking stress, baby – I can do without it. He fell asleep in his chair.

Narcolepsy.

Inspector Hedge had a name for it. It can last for a few seconds or several minutes, occasionally longer. Untreatable. He waited. Johansen shuddered, blinked, jerked his head back and opened his eyes.

How long have I been asleep?

About a minute.

It could have been a century. I was in a green forest. Deep in the forest with the bears who are quite friendly believe me. I always go there. To the forest. It is an alternative universe to me. Sometimes I think – hey – you don't live here you live in the forest and the rest you dream. My brother? What do you think? He is in the forest?

9

By the time Albert Hess had reached the hotel in Reykjavik Mr Green had checked out. Hess had said, Taxi! I have come to collect a fare, Mr Green.

It's a wasted fare, I'm sorry. It must have been a double booking, said the female receptionist. Nice looking with a blonde pony-tail. Maybe she's into S and M, thought Hess appraising her. You could never tell from appearances.

Sorry, your Mr Green has already been collected, she said.

Oh. Was that by my associate – a guy – how can I describe him...?

Athletic build, blond hair? Supplied the girl. She was not a bad looker, been round the block but knew how to look after herself. No rings on her fingers.

That's him! He said.

He's a star, answered the girl. Or woman. When do you start calling a girl a woman? She was still talking, listen to her.

Some time ago, she said. He was an ice hockey national champion. Everyone knew his name – Gisli Johansen! That's him for sure. But he had a bad injury and that finished his career – and then a few reports of rowdy behaviour and eventually a prison sentence for drunk driving. Then nothing. He disappears from view. That's how it goes.

Tell me what I don't know, said Hess with a laugh. He's one of the best! A heart of gold! But that guy has just taken my ride.

You need to take it up with your Head Office.

I will do that, said Hess. You don't happen to know where they were going?

The same place as you were booked to take him I guess, said the girl. Too smart for her own good.

Yeah, you must think I'm dumb, eh? You know what? Some clients change their destination. They want to go further but they want the same price. Or they just change their mind.

Well where were you to take him?

I'm not taking him! But I didn't know that. I had to cover the job – for your ex-national hockey star on ice – Johansen, right? I had a bad night – out on the town – give me a break please, my brain cells are still celebrating.

Then you're lucky you are not driving all the way to Isafjordur.

I sure am. I better go home and sleep. By the phone in case I get another job.

OK. Good luck... The receptionist picked up the phone to answer an incoming call and Herr Albert Hess had got the information he needed. But he still wanted to fuck the girl. He wanted to do more than that and his antenna told him she would play. Amazing, wasn't it, what the bitches really wanted? He waved. She waved back. He walked out into the night reminding himself that bad habits could cost him his employment. She could wait. He would be back.

When he had arrived the Airport Hess had managed to hire a Mercedes-Benz 300 SL with fuel injection and a very good top speed. It was a luxury hire he knew that – on the Firm – but they had not complained about his expenses so far – he was worth it. He had a high kill-rate. Some of them it was true were off the books but a man like him needed to keep his hand in. Particularly he regretted that his assignments had not included any women, however he had been able to balance that up a bit but he had to be careful because Head Office would not approve if they knew. Then again what did they not know?

He climbed into the Mercedes coupé which was parked outside the hotel and smelled the leatherwork with affection. He appreciated good things. People would say, oh I would kill to have that! And that's exactly what he had done. Albert reached into the glove compartment and took out a roadmap of Iceland and found Isasfjordur. He checked the petrol gauge, the tank was as good as full. He put on his worn soft leather gloves. Life was good. He turned on the engine that purred back at him like a kitten. He took off the handbrake let in the clutch and was soon outside Reykjavik, heading north.

Albert Hess was pleased with himself. He had got on to the track of this Mr Green quickly after being diverted. It was only a few hours ago – he had just got back home from Tempelhof after a fruitless wait for the bloody Mr Green – hardly put his foot inside his apartment door when the phone was ringing and it was Head Office directing him to return to the Airport – this time to take a flight to Reykjavik – to pick up his travel documents at the Icelandair desk. And... but never mind, he knew what he had to do.

The car lights were on cutting into the brief damp night of this embarrassment to geography, a place called Iceland. Not worth invading, don't waste your jackboots here comrade! This was as dark as it got in this crazy country that sold fish and had a nascent banking industry. Banking was all about imagination. It was an act of faith. Perhaps one day he would become a banker – at a certain age being an assassin was not such a good idea. He had fallen into the profession. In 1945, after the collapse of Germany, as a member of the SS he did not rate his prospects of survival highly. He had been taken out of a POW cage and interrogated by a Colonel Brown of US Army Intelligence. The Colonel must have had a quota to fill – on a need to further employ. SS Obersturmfuhrer Hess was amongst those put on trial on reduced charges and sentenced for war crimes but he knew it was nominal and that he would be released quickly into the service of his new paymaster. Those who yielded the Yankee Dollar. He guessed CIA but nobody gave him a name. Say this for Iceland, the women were interesting. He guessed they had their own way of keeping warm.

10

Inspector Hedge sat up upon the bed while his companion slept across the small divide on his own single bed. This was all that was available or perhaps a better means of protecting him. The Icelandic, slightly less than giant in proportion, did not look like he was cat-napping, he was out for the count. That Hedge had this clown looking after him did not bode well even if the aforesaid idiot could spout poetry. Not that he thought he was in any particular danger. But then the next minute he did think he was in a very particular danger.

Hedge had completely revised his opinion of this mission – so called mission – who called it that apart from him? The truth was he had been sent on a wild goose chase. They – yes, them – had wanted the Inspector out of their hair so they had cooked up a trip abroad and whether he had stayed in Berlin and followed the storyline they had doubtless prepared for him, to keep his mind occupied, or that he had fled to Reykjavik was of no real consequence to them whoever they were. The fact that he, Inspector Hedge, had imagined he was in danger was all to the good, he had swallowed the bait hook line and sinker. So here he was in another narrative, they were indulging him. They liked games.

They were practising on him. They were trivialising him. And worst of all they were laughing at him. He could hear them. Now. Bellowing with laughter following his antics! They were practising control of a subject – it was probably a student project – getting your new wet-behind-the-ears boys and girls in MI6 to dip their toes in the muddy waters of espionage. That's what it bloody well felt like to him and Jack was not given to swearing. He was a field exercise.

He was an odd bod from the Met, a rogue policeman lent out by his Super, a traitorous friend. He was seconded without his knowledge surplus to requirements – oh come on that's a fudge! He was a clear and defined threat to the Establishment and they had to degrade his capabilities. They had closed down his last case, stop rocking the boat!

The phone rang. Hedge reached out to take it. Gisli swung his legs off the bed and grabbed the phone. Yah...? Yah... Yah, OK... He hung up and lay back upon the bed propping his head up with the pillow. He nodded. Like I said, my friend, it's a shit storm. We must make the best of it, yah? That is what we are paid for. The Icelander looked infinitely sad.

Hedge said, Your employers speak English?

What are you expecting? It is an international language and this is an international operation. You are aware of that, Mr Green? What are you aware of? I do not know. You like a good poem, nothing else I know, nothing else I need to know. Personally I am most upset for the way this is turning out. It is a farce. Fuck them I say. They own my time they do not own my soul. They expect me to kill you? To put a bullet in your head or dispose of you in any way I please but do not leave a trail back to Head Office. Oh no I am not paid for that. I used to play ice-hockey. I was pure dynamite. I was pure energy. What happened to that guy?

You have instructions to kill me?

Precisely. I am sharing with you my dilemma. You should be upset too, Mr Green. Here I am sitting next to you masquerading as your pal and my job is to dump you in one of the fiords? Yah shit happens they tell us – but I quit!

What about the trawler? Inspector Hedge was not convinced. Was this another game?

The trawler?

That I am supposed to be catching? To go to Norway?

You can forget that, Mr Green. Is there a trawler? How the hell should I know? Or rumours of a trawler? Why would we need a trawler, Mr Green? There has been a change of plan. I tell you I would never have taken this job on if I had known what was expected of me.

So... what are you going to do?

I told you, Mr Green. I quit. I do not assassinate a fellow poetry lover. That's it. And oft when on my couch I lie, in vacant or in pensive mood, that's me. The fuck I'm going to kill someone. Would you? What would you do?

I would not murder. In self-defence I might have to kill.

Where does self-defence start? Is it an economic proposition? Is it a matter of having two ex-wives to maintain and three kids? Everyone needs money.

They will come after you, said Hedge. You know too much.

So? There will be two of us – two of us to come after? We are both armed – armed and dangerous, eh? I have switched sides. I am at your service, Mr Green.

Gisli lit up a cigarette.

Hedge said, You realise the dangers of secondary smoking – you might at least ask my permission.

Gisli jumped up. So sorry! I will open a window. He opened the window and returned to the bed. There was an ashtray on his bedside cabinet. He inhaled deeply and stubbed the cigarette out. I am so bloody sorry Mr Green for endangering your life by secondary smoking. Perhaps that is the way I can assassinate you? It will take longer. He started laughing.

Calm down, Mr Johansen.

Gisli...

Have you killed anyone else?

What?

Before?

Yes, but the guy was a bastard. It was easy. Someone had to it. You know, like when you have the moral imperative.

They won't let you go. You know that?

Silence.

Johansen started reciting,

    Quinquireme of Nineveh from distant Ophir,

    Rowing home to haven in sunny Palestine,

    With a cargo of ivory,

    And apes and peacocks,

    Sandalwood, cedarwood and sweet white wine.

John Masefield, said Jack Hedge and took up the recitation,

    Stately Spanish Galleon coming from the Isthmus,

    Dipping through the Tropics by the palm-green shores,

    With a cargo of diamonds,

    Emeralds, amethysts,

    Topazes, and cinnamon, and gold moidures.

Letting the resonance of the words bring the bracing taste of sea spray to their lips they recited together the last verse,

    Dirty British coaster with a salt-caked smoke stack,

    Butting through the Channel in the mad March days,

    With a cargo of Tyne coal,

    Road rails, pig-lead,

    Firewood, iron ware, and cheap tin trays...

How do I know you won't change your mind, said Hedge. All things considered?

You don't, said Johansen. Let's go for a swim.

In the motel pool in the water of the fiord they swam together naked for they were the only ones about. Later as the shock of the cold water gave way to a sense of euphoria it was time to emerge and put on warm white bathrobes and sit on the loungers by the pool.

It's great to feel well again, said Gisli. My strength has returned after my fight with alcohol and drugs. I gave in. I could not win. It started with pain-killers for a broken leg then it happened again and more drugs... Anyway I finished up in jail where I got into recovery.

You still drink?

Only the occasional beer. So far so good.

It's never interested me, said Hedge.

Gisli lit up a cigarette. You know once on another job I got a call – a telephone call – to dispose of this guy – you know – and then half an hour later I got another call cancelling the contract. Luckily I had not even started the work. Apparently this often happens. Head Office is not a monolithic voice but a hotbed of confusion. They are having a reshuffle.

While there's life there's hope, said Hedge. Don't you have a number you can call them?

I have an emergency number. I am only to call it as a last resort.

You could give me the number. Hedge nodded agreement with his own sentiment.

Gisli frowned. What's the point of that?

Well if something happened to you I could phone them and let them know.

What could happen to me?

You never know. It's risky business we're in.

Gisli laughed. You are pulling my legs!

It's one leg, Hedge corrected him.

You are pulling my one leg?

Yes. You see – how can I put this Mr Johansen...?

Gisli.

Right. I don't believe Head Office want me deleted. And I'm not just saying that because it suits me not to be deleted, you understand? Which is natural. No, not the new organisation, they're on my side. There's a power struggle going on, you're right, on the Top Floor of the non-existent Office. Actually it's a fight between good and evil, so corrupted I'd go so far as to say that some are in league with the Devil.

That's heavy stuff man.

Yes. They're the ones that want me out of the way. You see...? Yes, I'm a threat to them. We should hang on for another phone call.

Gisli tapped his feet. OK. Don't get nervous. It's contagious, man.

Only – only I thought – in the pool – just now – for a moment – I thought you were going to – to try to drown me.

I am so much stronger than you, Gisli replied. That would be a good way to do it, eh? I thought about it too – did you see it in my eyes? He laughed again. I asked myself what would I be throwing away on a stranger? My fucking livelihood man! The welfare of my kids – I would be mad! We've all got to go sometime. Drowning is common for Icelanders – the sea, the sea! It is something we accept. He stood up. How about one more dip? It is totally therapeutic. He let his bathrobe fall off. His body was still in good shape – for a recovering addict very good – even if he would never play ice hockey again.

OK. Hedge stripped off his bathrobe. I'm game.

Good. Last one in the water's a sissy.

The Icelander pushed Hedge in the pool. He laughed as Hedge came flailing to the surface.

So I'm the sissy, eh?

He dived in and came up close to Hedge and murmured,

It would be so easy. To do it now...

He grabbed Hedge by the shoulder. Listen, Mr Green, who's to say you didn't have a heart attack? I'm fucking crazy you know! You know? That's my problem man! Fucking crazy! It would be so easy...

Hedge spluttered, OK you've had your fun. That's enough...

Fucking crazy! Johansen had hold of both of Hedge's shoulders.

But you won't do it...

You mean it's erotic? A male bonding thing? Eh? Let's see, shall we? He pushed Hedge under the water. The man's strength was irresistible. Hedge below the surface struggled. He was not enjoying this game. He must not panic. The damn fool would tire of his joke soon – better not to struggle. Peering up he saw the water turning red. The grip on Jack's shoulders loosened and he broke to the surface as Johansen floated away. The carmine lake expanded around his inert body as his spirit was greeted by his already departed brother. They did not tarry on the scene. By the poolside pistol in hand stood Herr Hess.

Get dressed Mr Green, he said. We need to leave here quickly.

11

They were driving north, fast, in the Mercedes. Albert Hess prided himself on his skill behind the wheel. He had toyed with becoming a racing driver at one time but the war... yes the war and all that... His father had been killed on the Russian Front – that was the story – so naturally his mother had turned to him her only child and... and yes and so on...

So on and on...

Grief takes many forms, fanaticism being one of them. That his father – Vater – had died a hero and not a war criminal dear Vater – Heinrich – unapproachable – unimpeachable – his medals a shrine with candles lit every day in front of a silver framed photo and all that shit that he had gone along with for her sake – for her sake... Actually Colonel Heinrich Hess had served on Adolph Hitler's General Staff and had not died on the Russian front but had been shot for being part of the attempted coup against the Fuhrer (lucky not to have been strung up with piano wire) but never mind – that had been airbrushed from the mind of Mutter – dear Mutter so close to insanity but perhaps this illusion – along with all the others – had saved her from the asylum! Yes grief takes many forms and here he was earning a crust – well the whole damn loaf and he had plans to get out of this way of life and open a garage and who knows marry and have kids – not too late for that... Women! Who would put up with his habits? His nocturnal wanderings – his need to use the incinerator in the middle of the night – mind you marriage was a good cover and anyway he was capable of affection, yes. No, not sentimentality – real affection – love – of family and children – kinder, yah – goodnight princess sleep tight – he could have all that... He felt a pricking behind his eyes. Tears were forming. He often cried for little reason, how do you explain that?

Hedge spoke, interrupting his thoughts, You didn't need to do that.

What, Herr Green?

You were too quick on the trigger.

He was not drowning you, that man? What else do you call it?

It was too early to tell. It was horse play.

Horses in the water, yah?

Perhaps.

Listen, you want to know about Johansen? He was a heroin addict.

Johansen told me he had stopped.

He had stopped many times, yes. It never worked for long. I read his file. A copy was given to me at Tempelhof Airport. I read it on the plane to Reykjavik. Everything was in a hurry you understand? You tried to give us the slip, yah? But it was good for the brain cells – we needed to respond quickly – that was good. Sehr gut. You provided us, Mr Green, with an emergency exercise – switching countries – switching stories – it has all been accomplished, yah! Very good – sehr gut, mien Herr. And by turning it into an opportunity Head Office decided it was time to delete Mr Johansen, you understand? You spent time with him – you know he was how do you say? Flaky? Yah, flaky! He had become unreliable – extremely unreliable – you bet! You bet your bottom dollar!

Inspector Hedge was not convinced. It was his job to let the suspect convince him. If this man Johansen was already carrying out instructions to kill me – orders from your Head Office – why did you stop him?

Because I had different instructions. Is that not obvious?

Why would your... people, give contradictory instructions? From the same source – one to take me out? And the other to rescue me?

Listen, Mr Green, in a perfect world this would not happen. No way. But this an example of bureaucratic bungling! Yah? Yah, I think so! We must not worry, it will be straightened out.

You think so? Where did the error lie? With the instructions given to Johansen? Or the instructions given to you?

Hess replied cheerfully, I do not know. You can scratch your head on that one or we can have a nice day! You want another scenario, Mr Green? Maybe whoever was running Johansen was not running me. It can happen. Different desk. Different paperwork. You imagine that all Western Intelligence Agencies are working together? Not on your life, buddy! It turned out well for you – why are you complaining? You have a shitload of hours ahead of you. For the time being everything is OK – hunky dory, eh? You are alive – and I am alive – how good can that be? The rest will be ironed out, as you say. It will all come out in the wash, eh? You bet! You bet your bottom dollar!

Jack Hedge was still in shock. He did not like people being killed around him – to see above him the water in the pool turning red while he surfaced to take a deep breath and the red red wine of his companion's life was spreading across the pool. He tried to reconstruct the event. Had Johansen actually loosened his grip before the shot? Had he Hedge heard vaguely a shot or was he instituting it now into the grisly scenario? The point being...

Was Gisli done with his game – if it was a game – before the murder? His grip relaxing? A quite un-necessary murder except that this bloke who had turned up – this German Herr Hess who now posed radically as his saviour – this Nazi if he read him right – was only carrying out orders to take out Gisli Johansen who had become flaky – unreliable – volatile. A bloke who spouted poetry no less. According to Head Office. His Head Office. The Hun! Which could be any one of a number of agencies – put that on one side for the moment – this bullet headed killer showed no remorse. Showed nothing...

Was he to be next on his kill list? Why delay if that was the case? Only because Head Office – the Top Floor – his People – not Johansen's People – had bungled the job – one desk not knowing what the other desk was doing and it would only have taken a tap on the door to compare notes – but they had their own way of working and producing their own SNAFUs...

He could take out his gun and hold it to the head of Herr Hess but what instructions would he give him then? Perhaps this impersonal force of nature sitting beside him driving with such expertise at high speed was indeed his saviour and Gisli would have proceeded with the drowning...

Let events unfold. Life would tell him. Thank you Granny for those words. For now he was in a story and in danger which gave him more sense of being alive. Of being Inspector Hedge. Perhaps the whole scenario was orchestrated to confuse those on the ground. But his head was clear – he was not suffering from hallucinations. Farewell Mr Johansen – Gisli – funny name – Icelandic name – you have returned to your green forest and the bears and left us to inhabit your dream. And when you awaken we will disappear.

The Mercedes sped onwards – north. Someone was in a hurry. Doubtless to get away from the scene of the crime. But how difficult could it be for the Icelandic Police to intercept them? Inspector Hedge had knowledge of these sort of things. Unless the local crime unit had been given orders from Higher Up to go slow – not an impossibility – a road block should be in place by now and there it was. Up ahead. They were flagged down and joined the queue of light traffic waiting to go through. A policewoman came up to the Mercedes as Hess lowered the window.

What's going on, Officer?

Where are you going?

North. Sight seeing. Hess smiled broadly up at the woman. Another ponytail blonde. Frisky. What he could for for her. He said, What do you recommend, officer? We are ignorant tourists – we are taking pot luck.

Your driving licence, sir. Where have you come from?

Reykjavik. Hess handed his driving licence out to the policewoman.

Did you stop on the way?

No. Not yet. This is our first stop.

She held the driving licence. Your passports, please. Both passports.

While they fumbled for their passports she asked another question.

What time did you leave Reykjavik?

Approximately 5am. An early start. I hope I have not broken any speed limits. Is this about that?

Was your passenger with you when you left Reykjavik?

Yes, we met at the hotel and decided to share a car hire and see the Westfjords together.

Hedge could see that Hess was angling in his seat to get into a position where he could draw his handgun. But he only produced from his clothing a passport and handed it out of the window. Hedge followed suit.

The policewoman studied both passports. She peered into the car. Can you confirm that story, sir?

Yes, I'm on convalescent leave, said Hedge. This is a holiday. I met this gentleman in the bar last night and we decided to spend a couple of days exploring together – sharing the cost of transport.

Hess pushed another document out of the car window. That is the car-hire agreement, officer.

The police officer was not finished. Did you notice anything unusual during your drive north?

Only the magnificent scenery! You are to be congratulated on it! Said Hess, a smile pasted on his lips. She handed all the documents back into the car.

Have a pleasant holiday, gentlemen.

They were through the police cordon and on their way.

Hess laughed. So you have more than one passport, Mr Green. Very convenient. Don't tell me which one you showed that pony-tailed bitch. She was asking for it, don't you think so? So many blondes – so many pony-tails – such high spirits to tame! Eh? Don't you agree? I must come back here on holiday soon. Very soon – if spared by God.

Do you believe in God? Asked Hedge.

Oh yes. Someone must carry out His divine retribution.

12

When did the whirlybird come? Shortly after that. Shortly after what? They were still some distance from Isafjordur, driving fast. Herr Hess had said...

When we get there, Mr Green...

What?

Or whatever passport name you are using today. OK, let us say Mr Green. It was Mr Green I was to meet at Tempelhof Airport after all but Mr Green took off to Iceland, did he not? Yah, so to protect Mr Green I had to follow which was as well because you are still alive. So I would like Mr Green to tell me... He let the words hang in the warmth of the leather scented air inside the car.

To tell you what? I have nothing to tell you, replied Hedge.

Without explanation Hess pulled the Mercedes off the road and on to the grass verge, braking to a stop. He turned off the engine. We are here, he announced. This is as far as I go without further instruction.

They alighted from the car. They stood taking deep breaths of the ice-scrubbed Arctic air and gazed down upon the Port of Isafjordur which nestled beneath them, picturesque and precise of contour in the sunlight.

Before we go down to the harbour, said Hess. I need to know something. If that is alright with you, Mr Green?

Like what, Herr Hess? How can I enlighten you? I could ask you questions. Like how a Nazi was recycled to become a security asset?

Herr Hess was seldom without a ready smile. He replied, That is true. We can ask each other questions all day. For instance you could give me a summary of your mission. I am at your service. I have run out instructions you see? I had to erase your recent pal who was a mortal danger to you – a careless involvement of yours – but I see you are not convinced? You do not see me as sympathetic. It is not enough I saved your life. Of course. You do not want to be in my debt. Understood.

Hess lit a cigarette, inhaled gratefully and continued, I am here to be your new best friend. I am here to protect you. Your last pal was a viper in your bosom. Anyway. Looked at another way this is not about friendship. I do not need a friend. I need orders.

Looking down upon the Port of Isafjordur Hedge wondered – could it indeed hold the next instalment of his story? This story of yours? How often had he said that to a sweaty suspect – it doesn't hold water son, this story of yours. How could he get inside the head of this piece of Nazi memorabilia from the last World War?

He said, I have no idea of my mission. No-one's told me that, Herr Hess. I thought you might be the one with news – or ideas on the subject.

That is a laugh, Mr Green. I am a foot soldier.

You want orders? You expect me to instruct you? After you bringing me this far?

Someone must. The ex-Nazi shrugged.

No. This one would never be an ex-Nazi, decided Hedge. There was no penitence in his make-up, simply the need to survive doing what he did best. He was hard-wired to kill. Hedge decided to offer him a few morsels though that was all he had to offer. The German did not need to know that.

I was driving to Isafjordur with Johansen. It was his instructions for Mr Green – but I told him – I said I'm not that Mr Green.

Then why did you go with him?

He expected me to. He didn't care which Mr Green I was, so... why not?

Hess turned to Hedge. You want to fence with me? I have no ideas. Are we going to stand here all day? What happens when we go down into the Port? Who are we looking for?

I'm not in touch with your Head Office, Herr Hess, so how would I know? I was relying on you to suggest the next move.

Unfortunately not, Mr Green. You have your own Head Office which does not exist? We know that. Of course of course. You have your own People.

No, regrettably I do not have any People. All I've got is you. Since Johansen – my guide and travelling companion that you so hastily despatched – has departed for the dark green forest and the friendly bears.

Bears? I have never found bears to be friendly, answered Hess, reflectively. Demoralised, yes. What bear would not be demoralised if their zoo was blitzed by the Allies and it had to wander the burning streets of Berlin looking for food?

Hedge did not buy the bears' hard luck story. He said, Johansen was supposed to take me to a trawler. He told me those were his instructions.

To go where?

Hedge did not answer.

There are plenty of trawlers down there in the harbour. Look. Which trawler had you in mind?

I don't have trawlers in mind.

Put it another way, Mr Green. Who is your contact in Isafjordur?

I don't know. Johansen must have had some idea but he's dead. I do not have any instructions to pass on.

Hess frowned. He was irritated. He said, I know you are not telling me everything.

Hedge replied, Then you must know more than I do.

This is total shit! Shouted Hess. We are here in the field and no-one is able to issue an order? It is a fucking disaster, Mr Green! We are up shit creek without a paddle...

Hedge was enjoying the German's discomfort.

We can go down into the town – book into an inn on the quayside and wait for them to contact us.

Hess nodded. Them? Yes, all of them. You are the one with several identities, currently Mr Green, perhaps you are all of them. Who is in charge? I am the office cleaner. You have a mess, I clean it up. Can you please give me an order? We go down into the town of Isafjordur – yah? Is that an order?

Do you need orders?

Before the battle, yes. But during the fighting in the Waffen SS every rank was ready to take responsibility at the next level up – because anything can happen – we were trained to be sideways effective – not hierarchical. Not like the British Army resentful of senior ranks but lost without their command. Your Tommies were like headless chickens cluck cluck cluck...

I'm glad you got that off your chest, Herr Hess. Worth mentioning we chickens won the war.

The war against the Bolsheviks has still to be won, declared Hess. Which is why we are here. I await your orders.

Hedge looked down at the stillness of the port as if searching for an answer. He said, Here's what we are going to do, Oberleutnant. We are going to retreat from Stalingrad before we are encircled by the Russians.

Hess laughed and ground his cigarette out under his heel. He slapped Hedge on the back. Now that I like! That is your British sense of humour! You laugh and brew up another cup of tea – typical Tommy!

Hedge stared at the man, trying to penetrate his head. Surely he knew more than he was letting on. How could he tease it out of him? He said, A small point, Johansen asked me if I was circumcised.

Hess answered carefully. I did not kill Jews during the war. I have been cleared of all major war crimes at Nuremberg. I knew that things were going on around me in Poland – in Ukraine – in Russia – perhaps despicable things – but I was a soldier – I was obeying orders. My attitude to Jews is neutral. What was your answer to Johansen? Did you tell him you were circumcised or uncircumcised?

You are taking an unhealthy interest in the state of my penis, Herr Hess.

Do not worry – I will work with a Jew. Mr Green, I know your mission. You are to proceed to Norway to meet certain people in scientific circles to arrange the purchase of heavy water for Israel. My cards are on the table. I am to support you. So the Jews are building an atomic bomb, a fact which they will deny forever. Does this mean I am working for the Jews now? Am I a cleaner for them? Listen I get paid. My questions are lost in the air...

It was then the whirlybird came, chopping up the air into noisy pieces that fell upon their ears as it approached and descended sweeping the green shimmering grass in outward waves to settled into a meadow. The Superintendent was first out of the machine.

Inspector Hedge! What the devil are you playing at? You were supposed to go to Berlin! Who told you to cash in your ticket and come to Iceland? Or was it your own idea? Dragging everyone behind you at great expense! You have created an administrative quagmire! You are an utter menace! Get in! Get in! And you Herr Hess! You are included in the package! In you go! We are evacuating this scene! And that means NOW!

An operative in helmet and flak jacket ran out from under the slowly rotating blades to the Mercedes. Chivvied and pushed, Hedge and Herr Albert Hess ducked under the chopper blades and climbed up into the helicopter. The Super waited for the operative to return and pushed him aboard. Other hands pulled the Super aboard as the blades spun and the machine lurched like a lame bird that could no longer escape the cat. The helicopter thrust itself skyward...

As they ascended Hedge looked down. The car exploded in a ball of orange flame and smoke drifted up towards them. The scene shrank and vanished from view. Someone thrust a flask of coffee into his hands and he drank gratefully of the hot sweet liquid and felt it hit his stomach. He looked across the cabin at the operative who removed his helmet. But it was not a man. It was Margaret. His vision blurred. He blinked and as his focus swirled and returned and he was sitting across from Inflatable Policewoman Doris. And. And after that. But that was all...

13

He was in a forest. A dark green forest. And there was a figure up ahead of him moving through the trees. He could not be sure but he thought it was Doris. This was the forest of the singing bears. Gisli had not told him that the bears sing but it stood to reason that if they were friendly why would they not sing? The bears were shy but they would appear when least expected. He tried to keep up with Doris – if it was Doris – or not too far behind but he kept tripping over the roots of trees that were deliberately putting them in his way. The trees were not as friendly as the bears but if you were being cut down, the forest being diminished relentlessly, would you be so friendly? He could not keep up. He could not keep up with his own thoughts. He could not keep up with Doris who bobbed along and disappeared ahead. He sank down into soft mossy topsoil and rested. Doris, yes say it was her, she could go her own way. The bears could come. His one big worry was that they would run out of the forest of trees, that they would be no more. In other words though words were precious and should not be carelessly used in such a manner as finding several ways to describe the same thing – words were like water a scarce resource in the forest and should be saved for lyrics of the bears' song when they arrived as they undoubtably would. He might have fallen asleep but he probably was asleep so that would not work. All that falling asleep would do would bring him back to another world – one that he suspected existed and that he was happy to escape from and to be instead in the forest with the bears. But where were they? He waited, breathing. He waited, listening. He heard a rustling in the undergrowth. He was worried that they were near a motorway and that the forest would end and that would also be the end of the bears because unless they could walk and sing in the endless forest they would become extinct. But he could not worry about everybody. That was not his job. He was not a bear minder. A bear warden. He was not really anything because he did not have a uniform and a bear warden would have a uniform or at least a badge. Or a hat. Or a net to catch naughty young bears who ran out into the road. There they were. Five bears poking their heads through the bushes through the trees through the foliage. They started to sing:

We are happy happy bears!
Happy happy bears!
We are living in the trees,
Chasing honey bees
Doing as we as we please,
In this our life of ease...

We are happy happy bears!
Happy happy bears!
Chasing honey bees,
Until running out of trees
Running on the motorway,
That's a place we dare not stay,
That's a place we dare not play,
That's a place where babies die,
Making Mommy Bear to cry,
Making Daddy Bear to moan,
Winding up a gramophone...
Tralalalalaa...

We are happy happy bears!
Happy happy bears!
We are dancing in the stars,
Twanging our guitars,
Baby bear struck by a comet,
Causing Mommy Bear to vomit,
Causing Daddy Bear to moan,
Winding up the gramophone,
Tralalaalalaa...

We are happy bears!
Happy happy bears...

Inspector Hedge opened his eyes. He was in a white room. He was lying in a hospital cot but he was not strapped down. He felt his arms, he was not on a saline drip nor were electrodes attached to his body. All these non-happening things he regarded as a bonus though how he came to be in this white white room he had no idea. He sat up leaning on one elbow and stared across at the other bed. Upon it bounced an inflated policewoman but it was not Doris. This was a more recent model and not a patched-up one – a new model – one with which he was not so familiar.

The Superintendent entered the room. Hello, Hedge. I've brought you some grapes. He sat down on a chair by the bed and leant forward. How the devil are you, my favourite Inspector? No, don't sit up. Conserve your strength. You have been leading us a merry dance and that's for sure.

I was drugged, said Hedge.

Obviously. For security reasons.

Where am I?

You are in a clinic, Jack. Where your state of mind can be monitored.

Which country?

Iceland. Look out of the window. Where you bunked off to, you damn fool. Dragging the rest of us after you. Is it too much to ask you to obey your written instructions? You should have gone to Berlin. Never mind that now, for your own good we have paused you.

Hedge pulled himself up to a full sitting position in the bed. He said, I don't see how your policy of employing inflatables will pay off. They are an encumbrance. An emotional hazard.

If I did know what you were talking about, Inspector – which I do not – I would still advise you to mind your own business and play the cards dealt to your hand.

You can't put the Inflatable Policewomen back on general release. They are too vulnerable, sir. It won't work.

Change the subject please, Jack, or we'll never get you out of here.

You mean I'm hallucinating? Hedge queried. That would make sense. Put it another way, Lenny, as you are here – apparently – and not in a cottage in the woods eating the three bears' porridge – is someone outside trying to kill me?

Of course they are. To them you're contaminated.

Contaminated as in the Black Plague? By a biological agent Code Name Green Swan?

No, I don't want you to think like that, Jack. That's the crux of your problem. You are contaminated by your thoughts. By your thinking. Your thinking to them is dangerous – contagious! Highly contagious!

To them?

Yes, them. Who else? What's in your head is toxic, Inspector. It needs getting rid of – deleting – expunging. Put bluntly your thinking must be contained before it becomes a leaking security problem.

Is that your opinion?

It does not matter what my opinion is. Relax, you have friends. You still have friends. Have a grape.

Inspector Hedge refused the offer and waited for his superior officer to continue.

After your last case it was decided by some in MI5 that you posed a deep security risk with the information that you had come by. I was given a tip-off to get you out of the country for a little while, away from elements, which – how shall I say – would rather you were taken out. By Heaven I'm not going to lose one of my best men. A man whose erratic thinking can solve the most obtuse of cases.

Why couldn't you have told me all this before?

You stripping off in my office, Jack, destroyed the moment for any further intimacies. You got your marching orders through the post. With the help of other agencies we were going to hide you away in Berlin while we waited for the situation to develop back home and found the right moment to put you back into play.

On my original case? Hedge insisted. Of the plague cover-up?

The Superintendent was eating the grapes.

I say these grapes are good. They were flown in fresh today. Look here, old chap, it's the devil of a situation. You turning up in Reykjavik gave Section – which does not exist by the way – the opportunity they were looking for to get rid of you because they had by coincidence – or maybe not – a man on the ground in Iceland. They activated a story for you adapting it from a Mr Brown to a Mr Green – do you follow?

Of course. Inspector Hedge nodded. Into the woods...

The Super smiled. They – let us call them they – they enjoyed the sport! They have found that to let their assets sleep for too long is not a good idea – everyone gets rusty so they worked out a hypothesis, you understand? Something that could possibly be true – but may not be true – to test against the reality – if you'll excuse so vulgar a term – the reality of Cold War conditions. Most of these stories would run harmlessly alongside whatever was going on but occasionally – do you follow so far, Hedge? Good. Occasionally a cock-and-bull story they had invented and upon which premise they had set into action their assets – occasionally these assets would interface with what was actually going on. Add to it – mix in with it – and give us an advantage of insight into the intentions of hostile elements. Like Russia that could be helping Egypt, a country which does definitely not want to see Israel successfully developing an atomic bomb.

Is that happening? Asked Hedge.

We're not sure. But as you had turned up they decided to run you and see what happened.

Yes, well while I was running someone claiming to be working from Head Office tried to kill me while someone else claiming to be from Head Office rescued me. I am impressed by your grasp on these affairs, Leonard – you a cop – a career Metropolitan Officer with a firm grasp on promotional etiquette but... I am well but not well enough to be playing this game about a World War. Tactics that could blow up in the Middle East. Even if you discover that your exercise interfaces with a bloody reality!

Steady, Jack. Let's put it this way, there is one Head Office. But in any Head Office there are various Sections. And in the Sections there are Subsections. The atmosphere being of secrecy and confidentiality many of the Subsections do not know what the other is doing. This confuses the Russians! But it can lead to confusion in our own ranks. I do know that they are shaking the tree and the coconuts are falling out.

What do you want me to do?

Keep playing Mr Green and see where it leads.

It would have been easier for me to change to Mr Brown.

We couldn't get to you in time. It's no longer an exercise, Jack. There has been a Reality Interface. The hypothesis has turned into a theory that needs testing. I shall continue my grubby career-climbing which will either land me up in prison or the House Of Lords. Or both. And you – you will find your way from here on. You will receive pointers along the way. Once again you have stumbled upon something that could be vital. You have that knack. That homing instinct. Never lose it.

Hedge was not convinced. Nor was he satisfied. What about the last case, Lenny? People were dying because a germ warfare experiment went wrong and this virus could be getting into the community and who knows spreading across the world.

The Superintendent stood up. In that unlikely event the world will doubtless deal with it. This clinic to which you have been for your own safety will discharge you in the morning. You will proceed to London. You are officially re-activated as Mr Green.

Why did you allow me to be drugged on the helicopter?

To alter your perception of reality, Hedge. Any more questions?

Yes. Which Mr Green am I? The same Mr Green as left London? Or a different Mr Green?

How the hell should I know? You will find out. Goodbye, Inspector Hedge.

Hedge said, Hang on. Who introduced the latest inflatable policewoman model into my room? You can see it, can't you?

Your luggage is not my business, Mr Green. And by the way, Mr Emphatically Green, you will not be able to travel with this piece.

His chief produced the Walther PPK revolver.

Sorry. We need to get you home without complications. For the rest you can pack what you like, my dear chap. But do leave your hallucinations at reception. You won't be needing them.

The Superintendent left the room. The breeze of the door closing behind him set the inflatable policewoman bobbing gently up and down.

Hedge stared at his new partner forced upon him by Home Office economy measures. Give her a name – not Doris no more heart tugging associations – keep this professional. Alright, Lucy, where's your instruction manual? The point was could he trust her? With that bland assured expression that did not change? That seemed to invite the sort of confidences that detectives on a job together shared. OK let's get something straight shall we? Yes, because you are a new model, Lucy, off the assembly line and there are things I need to know which are not written in the instruction manual Lucy like are you recording my words? Are you videoing my actions? How can I switch you off? Who controls you? Your moods? Your affections? Lucy? Oh come on I am clear that I am talking to myself and was it ever different? Am I going under again? This must not happen – it's what they want – they want me to go to a dark place – where possibly they can meet me – but it's going to be on my terms where we meet – in which dimension, you understand? I must keep control. I must know the difference...

From a jug he poured himself a cordial and drank the glass down.

Policewoman Lucy intoned mechanically, Affirmative Action Is Required.

In half an hour he was packed, though packing did not include much more than deflating Policewoman Lucy and putting her into the bag provided along with the pump, repair kit and instruction booklet. Previously he had dressed provided as he was with a change of shirt, socks and underwear from somewhere. He left discarded clothes behind – he left his fear behind – the sweat in those garments – he left all except his partner now deflated who could have been spying on him – he left his story behind – though Mr Green would see him to the airport – a fragment of that identity would get him to Keflavik International Airport and through Security. One thing was clear he had no intention of pleasing them – whoever they were – and going to Norway to test the theory that Israel was determined to bring an atomic weapon to the heart of the cauldron of the Middle East...

And then what?

If Israel got the Bomb would Egypt take that lying down?

Behind Israel, America. Behind Egypt, Russia.

In Reception he checked out. No bother his bill had been prepaid. He ordered a taxi. There were a few clients drifting in and out going to the various thermal therapies and amongst them Inspector Hedge expected would be someone keeping tabs on him – take your pick who that might be – MI6, the CIA or Mossad?

Or the whole damn lot of them?

He had no clever plan to shake off a tail. He wanted to get home.

It struck him then, yes, he was returning to London. The next episode would be triggered – of his illness – or the drama of an unfolding case – because that's what policemen like him had – cases! Files, papers, documents and statements that could be altered because the needs of a case could vary long after the investigation proper had been concluded. Depending on the world of politics and what was deemed to be in the Public Good. The Public Good was important. Which could let's face it be changed or manipulated according to the weather.

The taxi driver was an ageing hippy smelling of weed who wore a wooden cross around his neck. Inspector Hedge climbed into the back of the car which had been freshened with a lemon spray and they set off. He had no way of knowing whether this was another would-be assassin or a mildly brain-damaged peacenik.

Where you going, man?

To the airport.

What, to meet someone? Like your Maker, yeah? We never know when that will be, right? Only joking, man! You travelling or what?

I'm travelling.

You don't have to tell me nothing, man. Like I mean anything – I can tell you're all clammed up like a seafood smorgasbord, right? I respect that, right? I mean you're paying, I'm driving. The point is man, Jesus, but hey I don't preach. You're an intelligent man, right? And you understand – what? OK! This cross – you see this cross...?

The hippy – or actor assassin playing one of his roles – lifted the cross strung round his neck meanwhile driving with one hand, fast.

This cross represents like – the lateral part, right? Is time – our journey through time, supposedly – that illusion, man, but – but the vertical part of the cross is our awareness in the moment – the transcendent moment got it? That releases us from the tyranny of time, mate! Of the Desperate Hours from which we are released! Along with Humphrey Bogart! The Desperate Hours, get it? The film man! Like the like movie?

Hedge had had enough of this guy. His dialogue was worse than a physical assault. Fortunately at this point the car turned off the motorway and they joined the slip road which was signed, KEFLAVIK INTERNATIONAL AIRPORT.

14

To Inspector Hedge the sound was like unto the bells of Heaven ringing as his Granny used to say. For Margaret sitting opposite to him was laughing. Her. She today, gone tomorrow, was his MI5 contact. Apparently. Apparently was all he had to go on. Margaret was debriefing him in the noisy Nine Elms pub underneath the arches at Vauxhall. She said, I'm glad that hairy hippy taxi driver gave you some prostate advice. He looked around the noisy crowded smoke-hazed saloon bar.

Is this where all the spies meet?

Yes darling we are in the right place. They can see us, can't they? But they can't hear us. Terribly frustrating when they've come all the way from Moscow. Actually, you see that couple over there?

She indicated a Eurasian woman sitting at a table some way off, a stunning ash-blonde woman with high cheek bones who could have stepped straight off a tractor out of a Stalinist poster announcing another record Soviet harvest.

Well she's a lip reader.

How can you tell?

It's the way she's paying attention to us.

Shall I wave?

No darling, don't spoil their evening. We have a protocol. Half of the spy game is actually giving the enemy information. What's the good of having a deterrent if they don't know how devastating it is? Beside which sometimes we are on the same side but we cannot officially recognise it so we pass information to each other like this.

Do the Russians need to know what I'm involved in?

They already know, don't worry about it.

What am I involved in, by the way? Perhaps they can tell us something I don't know. Like who was trying to kill me.

Nobody knows which side they are on today. It's a fight for survival at the higher levels – beyond subsection – which we do not know about except the grunts like us in the trenches are feeling the strain.

It's to do with my last case, isn't it? It's nothing to do with an Israeli atomic bomb programme.

Possibly...

She was smoking in the provocative manner that she had – like Claudette Colbert – but to Jack it was a noxious habit.

Please stop, he said.

What?

Smoking. It will get you in the end.

I'll be gone before then, she said. Her smile was painful and Hedge felt sad. What was she hiding? Did she even know? I joined the Force to keep the streets safe, he said. It was that simple.

Well they're not now and they never will be. Nor are the skies safe above the streets. You can forget all that stuff, darling. Life is inherently not safe, it's a matter of degree.

Isn't that cynical?

Oh come off it, Jack, we do our best. She leant forward and he smelt the musk of her scent. She spoke quietly,

Currently we are engaged in trying to stop the proliferation of nuclear weapons in the Middle East. Or some of us are – others believe that any nudge and wink that helps the Israelis get their Bomb is to be welcomed.

What do you think?

We won't stop them. It's too late. They have too many friends. As your report suggests, it's Egypt that's the problem. They will try to seek a balance of terror by developing their own nuclear weapons programme. That's a given.

I haven't written a report.

You don't need to. I'll write it for you. She leant back, reached for another cigarette then put down the packet again without taking one out. She gave Hedge a quizzical look. What?

I'd like to be returned to the Met.

That's not possible.

I've got a case that is not finished. It's going cold.

Well let it. It can ice over as far as I'm concerned and we can skate on it, darling.

You were involved in it – MI5 – you were in it up to your neck – you were in the damn mental home with me that had an incurable ward of toxic scientists and lab assistants dying off below basement level – are you denying it?

What do you want from me? An official denial?

I'm not trained in counter-espionage, Miss.

Your last case took you into that area, where your volatility – your sheer unpredictability – proved to be a valuable asset.

That was ignorance.

Like it or not, Jack, you're in. There is no turning back.

You do realise I'm on sick leave?

What's that got to do with anything?

Hedge frowned. Well... am I sick?

What do you think?

I have hallucinations. I saw you on the helicopter. You were the demolition girl who blew up the car – I thought – then you turned into something else. My coffee was drugged...

Jack, I was not there. And if I was there it still wasn't me. Nor I did I turn into an Inflatable Policewoman, darling. I would have remembered. And, yes, you are still subject to hallucinations but not enough to impede your functionality. If you are imagining inflatable policewomen, I hope you find them attractive.

What the hell are you suggesting?

I want you to get something out of it. It's a rotten job at times. It's lonely. Isolating. I should indent for an inflatable police detective – what a lovely idea! She laughed and smiled warmly at Hedge. Or an Inflatable Policewoman to keep me warm at night, that would be even nicer. For God's sake Jack, don't take it all too seriously. We want you to come off this alive.

We?

I. I do...

She laid her hands upon his. I'm on your side. You must keep going – the only way out is through. I'll be keeping an eye on things, don't worry.

Margaret stood up. Having received this morsel of comfort Hedge followed her through the throng of excited bipeds gathered at their watering hole for a good bellow and slosh on a Friday night.

Out on the street she turned to him, Bye bye, darling. She kissed him lightly on the cheek – hailed a passing taxi and disappeared into the night.

He thought he might walk some of the way for of all things he loved walking through a city – especially at night – his eyes and ears tuned for any disturbance. He could feel anger or resentment when it was nearby even in the buildings he passed. And when it was calm as tonight promised to be he felt a swelling of pride that people were enjoying themselves because they trusted the process of law and order. Yes, take a walk...

Hello!

Hedge turned. It was the the golden bombshell from the Record Soviet

Grain Harvest on the Russian Steppes.

You were looking at me, were you not? She had a foreign accent. I don't mind. Listen, if ever you need me? Who knows? From her Prada handbag she produced a card and handed it to him. The guy she was with in the pub waited for her in a BMW 700 saloon. After they had driven away Hedge studied the card. Upon it was inscribed the name, Zelda Debrovnik – Speech Therapist, with a phone number. He was not in the habit of picking up ladies in pubs but he put the card into his wallet.

15

Back in his Earls Court flat Inspector Hedge made himself a cup of tea. He was no further forward. He had been given an hallucinatory drug whilst in Iceland. Why was that? To reinstate his illness? Why call it an illness? He had glimpses – insights – doors of perception opening which Somebody Up There found invaluable. They had plenty of Plods, didn't they? While they grunted away with their in control appetites eroding gradually dully inevitably their senses with their nine-to-five commuting and endless crosswords to keep the brain cells banging uselessly away with little thought of the Cosmic Whirl in which we are all involved...

Why should he see his extraordinary perceptions as an illness? To say, Oh he's ill because he's different from us – he's cracked – not solid but broken and open to the influx of the timeless hunch – yes, it suited them to say he was ill. And sometimes it suited him to play at being ill. It had started as a child to get off school and the fearsome bullying – to gain a day's reprieve and to stay home with his mother – a sore throat would sometimes do it. Yes, he had played sick – but not looney – did it have its own progression?

When he had unpacked there was no inflatable policewoman. No Lucy. No conflict of interest between him and Doris rescued from the front window of a junk shop. Drinking his tea he stared across the room at the Inflatable Doris inscrutable of expression as she swayed gently back and forth upon the settee. She comforted him just by being there bobbing away no more than that. He felt drowsy...

He was in the forest and he knew that the bears were hiding in the green denseness watching him. There was no sign of Doris. Was this his story he wondered? Or would others claim it and evict him from the forest? Jack did not want to be evicted and decided to get on with it – after all the woods could be inhabited by many dreamers each one providing a strand to the tapestry that made up a Universe – a Universe that lay behind the forest. He decided to explore – to push through the trees and this was easy and pleasant – underfoot the earth was spongy and there were open glades that appeared suddenly letting in warm sunlight. Across one such glade he spied a glimpse of cloth – a dress – flashing legs, disappearing – and a haze of golden hair streaming behind the figure – gone! He hurried across the glade and plunged into the thickness of the trees again guessing where she had gone. He was fairly sure that it was Miss Debrovnik the speech therapist. Maybe she was looking for the bears to give them lessons in diction and to teach the Daddy Bear that is was wrong to eat his young – Baby Bear – even if he got very hungry – or angry – whatever it was that impelled the Big Bear to such an act. Perhaps jealousy over all the time Mummy Bear was lavishing on her young – didn't he himself know about that? The sudden anger of his father... He was stumbling now – he had lost her – then there she was – up ahead – another flash of golden hair! And once more disappearing. With renewed hope he followed – dodging trees – seeing her up ahead – then nothing – leading him on but maybe she was not aware of him. He hoped not. He wanted to spy on her – to know her secrets. Then she was entirely lost to him – this version of Goldilocks his own story. His own casting. What a brilliant idea to put Miss Debrovnik in that role... and there was the cottage in the clearing – like in the traditional story only this was his story and he had to tell it to find out what was going on. As he arrived at the clearing he was in time to see her enter the cottage and close the door behind her. He crept up to the window and making sure not to be seen himself peered into the room. The four bears – not three bears – were seated at the table eating porridge, Daddy Bear, Mummy Bear, and two Baby Bears! And seated at the the top of the table was Miss Debrovnik on a clandestine wireless set, sending a message. Concentrating. So she was a spy – as he had suspected all along – using the Goldilocks story as a cover...

Inspector Hedge was standing in the the bathroom holding on by an act of will his body shaking. In one hand he held a glass of water in the other a handful of sleeping tablets. The container lay open and empty in the sink. Why take one pill? Take the whole blooming lot or none at all. He stared into the mirror. He observed an unshaven man staring back at him – who was he?

Who the hell was he?

He moved from the sink and threw the tablets into the toilet bowl and flushed them down. Too late he remembered that he was contributing to the poisoning of the water supply – water that was being recycled and would come back in their taps. Already it was reported that because of all the drugs taken and passed as urine the Thames water was so contaminated that fish were changing sex. If even the fish were confused about their identity then he was not alone.

Jack Hedge had taken the uniform and joined the Boys In Blue to solve that riddle and now it was denied him. He had married to solve that problem and now he was divorced. His father he had not known since he was three. His mother was in and out of an institution in Yorkshire – what did being a son mean? His story had taken him inexorably into an area of pain and disorientation. He was fed up with being Jack Hedge. It was too nebulous. He was leaking into the boundless Universe in wave upon wave of anxiety. He had a passport in the name of George Green. Who was George Green? A commercial traveller in raw materials. What else? Was he married? Did he have kids? Was he a Dad? Was his mother sane? Had his father survived a death camp in Poland? George Green was an empty canvas – an unwritten page – there was no pain and no joy upon his countenance.

Why could he not become George Green?

He was aided in that fancy when the next morning another set of travel documents was thrust through his letter box. George Green was still required in Berlin. George Green was rebooked into the Hotel Herman on Behrenstrabe where he would be contacted.

Mr Green was back in business. That was a comfort to cling on to...

16

Herr Hess was in a phone booth at Tempelhof Airport trying not to shout and draw attention to himself though the door was shut as he addressed his near-deaf mother – or was she putting it on when it suited her?

Yah, Mutti! Yah, Yah! I am aware it is your Eightieth Birthday next Thursday visiting day! Yah, yah... Donnerstag! Yah, a coincidence yah, Donnerstag... Yah – Yah, I know you had me late in life – I was an afterthought yah ... You were not thinking at all? OK, no need to rub it in, Mutti... Yah, Yah, Yah... Vater was a predator but a very handsome husband,Yah! I will attempt to be there on your Eightieth Birthday, Mutti, circumstances permitting... Yah, I promise I will... What are you saying, Mutti? A surprise? Yah, it would be a surprise, Mutti, if I could bring along Adolph Hitler to your birthday party – for your Eightieth Birthday, Yah... Nein, I do not know which cave in Bavaria the Fuhrer is hiding preparing his miracle weapons, Yah... Yah and sending his sperm to South America – I do not know if he does that... Yah, I must go now, I am at the Airport ... I will not forget – how could I? Goodbye, Mutti... Of course I do, I am smothering you in kisses. Yah from head to foot – what more do you want from a son!?

Herr Hess hung up the receiver, yanked back the door and exited the phone booth. Who would have a mother like this? Adolph Hitler indeed – she was crazy! That explains it – she was crazy like all the other alte Frau in that venerable institution especially established for widows of High Ranking Wehrmacht Officers. No favours – even those who had tried to kill the Fuhrer were included – that was the strict condition of the Occupying Forces in allowing it to remain open.

His family had known the von Stauffenberg family – they were on visiting terms – that was enough to get his father shot though probably there was more to it than that. His own unblemished record in the Waffen SS had been enough to distance him from the shadows of the plot to assassinate the Fuhrer. He did have one black mark upon his record though one day he had refused to kill some Jewish children. He had told his Superior Officer straight that he would not shoot kids even if they were

Yids and they could get someone else to do their dirty work which they did. It had earned him a reprimand and possibly had gone in his favour as it was recorded in his file during his interrogation by the Yanks. The fact that he had slaughtered Jewish civilians, men and women, was overlooked.

He went to ARRIVALS and took out the piece of cardboard with MR GREEN written upon it. He was reasonably sure it was the same Mr Green that he had met in Iceland but there could be other Mr Greens, could there not? He surmised that Mr Green was Jewish. So what? He did not regard himself as particularly anti-Semitic. There had been a war, there had been an enemy. Now there was a Cold War and now there was a new enemy. Before there had been an Ideology, now it was just a living and enemies changed like a pair of underpants.

The plane was late. Hess retreated to a café and ordered a black coffee. He enjoyed its rich hot and dark taste which drove out of his mouth the abiding bitterness of wartime ersatz coffee. He had an envelope for Mr Green. And he had his own orders regarding Mr Green. He had saved that gentleman's life once – he wondered was it to take it at a later date?

Hello, Herr Hess?

Albert Hess swallowed his coffee and spluttered. It was his client. Mr Green. I am so sorry. Information was your plane was late. I am at fault. It is a court martial offence.

We made up time.

I could have missed you. I would not blame you for putting me on report, Mr Green. I hate lateness! Unreliability!

Forget about it. Inspector Hedge now Mr Green was all amiability. This man after all had probably saved his life. I recognised you of course. We have previous, Mr Hess, if you get my meaning?

Previous? Yah, that is so. Can I buy you a coffee, sir? Mr Green? As a small amend.

OK.

Hess ordered another coffee. He winked at the girl behind the counter. Make that two, Fraulein. And give me a call. You should be in films. As he paid for the coffees he took out a card, wrote a number on it and slid it across the counter. The girl smiled and pocketed the card.

Hess turned to his client. I get careless when there is a bit of skirt around, you understand? It is my fault. It will be the death of me one day. What a way to go, eh? Did you have a good trip, Mr Green?

Yes, thanks.

Welcome to Berlin, sir. There are entertainments here that I am sure will amuse you.

I haven't come here to be amused, Herr Hess.

That's a pity. Life is but a fleeting shadow.

Life's but a walking shadow, a poor player. That struts and frets his hour upon the stage, Herr Hess. And then is heard no more. I would not expect you to be familiar with the Bard.

It is a tale told by an idiot, supplied Hess. Full of sound and fury. Signifying nothing. He added, I much prefer Shakespeare to Goethe. He picked up Hedge's case. When you are ready, sir, I will drive you to your hotel.

Hedge indicated he was ready to leave and followed his driver this Herr Hess who as a recycled Nazi was now presumably employing his skills for the CIA. Mr Green had a driving licence amongst the documents provided to support his identity so presumably he could drive because so could Jack Hedge. Wouldn't it have been easier to let him hire a car?

We are of course being tailed, muttered Herr Hess. No, don't look back please. Let the Russians play their game. Inspector Hedge took him at his word. He did not look back as they exited the terminal building and headed for the car park.

The trouble with those guys, said Hess, is they see too many movies. They don't know how much it hurts until it is too late. He opened the rear door of a Mercedes saloon and Hedge got in and smelt the comforting and familiar smell of leather upholstery. After stowing the case in the boot Hess got into the car – put on his beloved black leather gloves and gave Hedge a smile in the rear view mirror. All ready to roll, Mr Green. I should warn you there may be a little action along the way. nothing that we cannot handle, OK?

OK, said Hedge. Let's go.

Herr Hess turned on the ignition and the engine purred into action immediately. He reversed the Mercedes out of the parking space drove to the exit of the car park and handed the attendant a ticket. Soon they were on the autobahn heading for the centre of Berlin. The traffic was light.

Hedge turned to look back. He could not make out any suspicious looking tail. Hess saw what he was doing.

Don't worry, I will tell you when they are coming. Relax. Did you have a nice trip? I have not seen you since Iceland. To tell you the truth – why bother to lie eh – I did not expect you to turn up today. I thought you might have gone to Baghdad.

Why Baghdad?

Why the hell not? It is an interesting place, but then so is Cairo. My father was with Rommel you know – he wanted to get to Cairo – it was more difficult in those days. Do you want to smoke?

No thanks.

Good. I don't smoke in the car. It is impolite to the client. He looked in the wing mirror. Ah, there they are – Laurel and Hardy, eh?

Hedge looked through the rear window and this time he saw some way back a motorbike, driver and pillion passenger.

They are waiting until the traffic is light, then they will come. You can lie on the floor if you like but you will miss the show. Most drivers try to outrun a tail like that. The trick is to let them come up on you and brake suddenly – then the fucking idiots are up ahead – confused – and you have them where you want them. Watch out Mr Green, here they come...

Hedge chose to watch the show. He was not armed so would not be able to retaliate. He wound down the window. He had an idea. Do you want to lend me your shooter?

Not necessary. Watch.

The motorbike came roaring up on them. Hedge could see that the pillion rider had a sub-machine gun at the ready. As they came abreast of the Mercedes Hess employed his pre-described tactics. He braked abruptly and the motorbike shot ahead. Not a shot had been fired yet. The guys were looking back, caught by surprise. Hess gunned the Mercedes coming up behind the bike. He pulled the steering wheel over and slammed the car into them – sending them skittering into the other traffic lane flying off the bike on to the tarmac. The journey was continued without further interruption.

Too many amateurs in the game, commented Hess.

I noticed they were Arabs, said Hedge. Not Russians.

Hess nodded. Yah, Arabs are better with the knife! This time it was easy for us.

17

The Hotel Herman. Hedge was in Reception signing in as Mr Green when he heard a familiar voice behind him,

Hello?

He turned to see Zelda Debrovnik. She said, Let's not waste time talking about absurd coincidences, please. I am in a hurry. Can you meet me in the hotel bar this evening at seven?

OK. Yes.

Good. See you then.

She gave him an extravagant smile that spoke of the Golden Wheat Harvest on the Steppes and fun amidst the hayricks. She exited through the revolving door. At the same time Hess was coming into the hotel. He looked back at the woman disappearing into the street. Then came forward to the desk.

Does that lady who just left stay here?

I cannot give details of guests, sir. The receptionist was young probably bisexual, a product of the post-war market in Youth.

Of course, I understand.

I am very sorry, sir.

There is no need to apologise. I am glad that there is a high degree of discretion at this hotel. It makes me feel safe.

Thank you, sir, the clerk simpered weighing up whether there was the prospect of extra earnings that night. He took the form from Hedge. And your passport, please, Mr Green. We will need to keep it in the hotel safe during your stay with us.

And if I require it for a trip? Say to East Berlin?

Yes, of course. We will return your passport to you any time you need it away from the hotel, sir. It will require another form to fill in that is all. He handed over a key. Room 515, sir. Can you manage your luggage or shall I ring for a porter?

Don't bother. Hedge picked up the case. He turned to his driver. Thank you, Herr Hess. You will no doubt be in touch with me.

Hess grabbed the case from him. Come on. This way. He led the way to the lift. Hedge followed. In the lift as it ascended Hess said, It is rumoured that this summer is to be very hot. Of course we have the lakes locally for swimming. Nice beaches and boating if you desire it.

Hedge said, I fear I have come too early in the season to take advantage.

Then we must entertain you with other pleasures that Western Berlin has to offer the tourist. They are of great cultural variety as our city enjoys the economic miracle afforded by the Marshall Plan.

The lift pinged at the Fifth Floor and they alighted and found Room 515. Inside, once the door was closed and securely locked, Hess shouted, What the hell are you doing!? I save your life a second time and you are trying to get rid of me?

Calm down, Herr Hess. Let me get you a drink from the mini-bar. Sit down, man. What's on your mind? You're over-stressed.

Hess sat on the edge of the bed. He produced a red coloured handkerchief and wiped his brow. Danke. Make mine a whisky. No ice. A little water if you please.

While Hedge served his room guest the room guest made it clear he was not in a hurry to leave. Hess kicked off his loafers and made himself more comfortable on the bed.

You cannot imagine the strain I am under. Now, because of that incident on the autobahn I will be called to account for the damage done to the Mercedes. No good explaining. They will say it is my fault. Bullet holes in the bodywork, that they will allow – because it is obvious – I should have let them shoot us up, yah? I will have to pay front right wing headlight smashed mudguard dented. They will declare it is careless driving.

I am a witness.

I cannot use you. It would compromise your position. How do I know you are circumcised?

I am not.

There you are. How am I to guess that? What do they tell me? The left hand does not know what the right hand is doing.

Hedge poured his own drink. That seems to be the theme of this operation. Cheers.

What are you drinking?

Lemonade.

Skoll.

They drank. Hess produced a book of receipts and a pen.

Sign here. It is a requisition order for a Walther PPK.

I didn't have to sign for one in Iceland.

This is Germany, mate. We are methodical.

Hedge signed the requisition order.

You must promise me not to leave the hotel. Not without me.

Not tonight.

Though your promise is worth nothing. It is made under duress so you have a get-out clause. Always read the small print when dealing with the English. They are snakes! A nation of shopkeepers! There we agree with the French.

Steady on, Herr Hess. You're getting ahead of yourself.

I will arrive for breakfast, Mr Green. Herr Hess slipped his loafers back on. Thank you for the drink. I can tell you it gets too much sometimes. It is not the killing though I do not know if we killed anyone today, I have not read the evening papers. You would not understand this – or maybe so if you have a mother – you see it is living up to her expectations – Mutti. She has her Eightieth Birthday this week – Donnerstag – Thursday. She has had so much disappointment. Our family have lost all their estates in Eastern Germany to the Russian communist swine. My father was shot by the Gestapo for his part in the 1944 plot to assassinate Hitler but she does not accept this. She is convinced he died on the Western Front – the Eastern Front – on any Front – how man Fronts can you die on? I told Mutti – Mother we were friends of the Stauffenbergs. She replies I don't know who they are. Can you imagine? We were in and out of each other's kitchens making strudels with the... Oh it does not matter. It is history now. Life moves on.

What are you doing for your mother's birthday?

That is the problem. I am at my wits end falling off the edge. All I do is try and please her but there is no way to please her. Hess took out his hanky and blew his nose loudly and wiped a tear from his eye. He stared at Hedge as though he might hold an answer.

She wants me to produce the Fuhrer at her birthday party.

What?

To invite Adolph Hitler, Yah.

I see. Is she in an institution, by any chance?

Of course.

Surprising as it may be to you, Herr Hess, I also have a mother and she is in a home – not quite for the afflicted.

Is she bewildered?

Yes. She does know who I am. Which is more than I do.

Thank you for sharing that. Danke. Good bye, Mr Green.

Herr Hess bowed slightly. Before leaving the room he composed his features once more into a familiar pattern or arrogance overlaid with a patina of humility. After all in World War Two though they had not won it against the might of the Allied cause they were runners up. It could be said that Germany came Second.

18

In the hotel bar that evening Inspector Hedge sat nursing a tomato juice with a dash of Worcester sauce, shaken not stirred. Rather like his state of mind. Actually it came down to this – he was expecting Herr Hess to ask him to dress up as Adolph Hitler to give his Mutti a lovely surprise on her Eightieth Birthday. Of course Hess was mad and he would refuse. Was this errant German related to another mad Hess, he wondered? Rudolph Hess, locked up in Spandau prison forever. It was not beyond the bounds of credibility that his nephew – Herr Hess could be a nephew – had a plot to break free his Looney Uncle – once the Number Two in Nazi Germany – who had parachuted into Scotland in 1940 looking for Lord Halifax and the Peace Party...

Hello again.

It was her! The adorable creature of light, Zelda Dubrovnik, from the Soviet Record Grain Harvest. He could hear the swish of nylons as she sat down opposite him.

Sorry I am late, darling.

For what? The day? The time of the month? The year? The point is you are here, Miss Dubrovnik. What would you like to drink?

Oh anything expensive, darling. A champagne cocktail perhaps. I don't mind. And some salted nuts. Without salt the limbs can give cramp and I have been sweating in the gym less than an hour ago imagine that?

Hedge could imagine it. He could imagine more than that.

How did you get to Berlin before me?

We are not fools! No, that's what the Germans say, isn't it? Not the Russians. She smiled at him. It was radiant. She was a Child of the Revolution, holding a bundle of golden wheat-sheaves against a setting sun, a blue handkerchief in her hair,

The waiter arrived. It was the same guy as had signed him in at Reception earlier.

Would you like to order a drink, sir?

How many jobs do you have in this hotel, enquired Hedge.

We are short staffed. Many young men like to work on the building sites where the money is good. The economic miracle is in progress but I am not strong enough to mix cement.

Bring the lady a champagne cocktail, please. And a bowl of salted nuts.

Anything for you, sir?

No.

The waiter left them to fetch the order

He was offering you sex, she said. This is West Berlin where anything goes.

I haven't come here for sex, Miss Dubrovnik.

A pity. You don't have to have come here for it but while you are here you might as well enjoy it.

That is a way of looking at life, yes. I take it that you have not come to Berlin for sex. What do you want?

To warn you, Mr Green. But what's the hurry? The night is young. Tell me, do you have any other plans for this evening?

Other than becoming involved with an attractive young woman who is working for the KGB? What is this? A honey trap?

You are already in a trap, Mr Green. A mouse trap. We are not hiding anything.

We?

Yes. Whoever you imagine we are. Sometimes our interests coincide and we want to get information to your people.

I was not aware that I have any people.

Come off it, darling. We all have people. I am trying to help you.

The waiter returned, served their order and disappeared.

You want to say I am KGB, she continued. I do not agree but I do not disagree that would make me disagreeable. I am also a human being and I do find you attractive Mr Green so why don't we enjoy our work? Because we never know when it will be brought to an end. Cheers, darling!

They drank.

Hedge said, Actually I don't have any other plans this evening, Miss Dubrovnik. What do you suggest?

You could take me to dinner on your MI6 expenses.

So that's what I am?

Whatever turns you on, darling. Let us make believe. To get us through the night.

19

They had moved on from dinner to an underground nightclub. Miss Debrovnik had gone to powder her nose or to phone her handler, possibly The Slab who reminded him of a concrete Moscow block of workers' flats. He was seated in a haze of tobacco smoke quite near a stage where transexual men danced divinely their costumes gorgeous the choreography first rate and so clever, mirrors giving the illusion that they were a large chorus.

By now they were on first name terms, he was George and she was Zelda. Yes let's make believe. Whatever gets you through the night. Truth to tell he was rather enjoying being George Green. He did not feel that he was impersonating anyone else, rather that he had found a new version of himself. He had discovered in himself a confidence that was like meeting an old friend long forgotten. He wondered how long he could remain George Green? No, that's a mistake, enjoy the moment. The exhausted weighed-down Jack Hedge version was gone – that was a relief – tonight he did not want him back – he did not want his anxieties – he did not want his commitment – especially he did not want his commitment to law and order. Tonight he was playing a part – he wanted it to get hold of him and to take him all the way. Inspector Hedge would have hedged his bets and played it safe...

Was he mildly pissed? Did George Green drink a little too much these days? There was a bucket of ice and a bottle of champagne by the table and that had cost MI6 a pretty penny – no doubt the entire budget of this operation – the mean buggers! He would have to indent for further funding in the morning, they could hardly refuse him. He was the cheese in the trap. The mice were nibbling. The mice were cunning. They would have the cheese and be gone before the spring had sprung...

The spring has sprung,
The grass is riz,
I wonder where the birdies is?
He giggled. There she was threading her way through the busy tables

and gaining admiring glances from even the women. As she sat down he could hear the silk moving, caressing her body.

She looked at him quizzically. Why are you laughing?

I had forgotten what it was like to have a good time.

She said, It is a time, darling, where there is no future that need concern us.

He added, Nor a past unless we like to invent it. He giggled again and poured champagne into their glasses then waved the empty bottle at the waiter, holding it upside down and pointing at it.

She said, this is on the KGB, George.

He intoned in a mock accented voice,

I once knew a man who loved an inflatable doll

They told him she would be good for a deflated morale

But when she was inflated

He got quite fixated

And would let no-one else ring his bell...

She said, You are coming from a weird place tonight, George.

Yes, he said, Where I have left behind a few people I can do without.

Zelda had stopped listening to him. She was looking towards the entrance where two men had come in. They were of North African appearance.

She said, George, we're leaving now.

The manager was approaching with another bottle of champagne. She stood up and gestured that it was no longer required and laid some notes on the table.

Come...

Hedge – was he Hedge now – was not so tipsy as George Green. He had no weapon with which to defend himself, or to defend her. He could see where the potential trouble lay. The two guys were staring at them. The only way out was to pass close to them. He remembered what Herr Hess had said about knives. He was alive to the situation. He was alive...

She was leading as they left their table. She said, Stay close. I can take those clowns down.

But Hedge would have none of it. He pushed ahead of her. She followed, her right hand in her silver Dior bag clutching a pistol. As they got to the exit one of the Arabs moved to block the way. Was it casual? There was a cigarette girl standing opposite to him – he picked up a packet of Lucky Strike, giving her money...

Hedge was totally alert – in the zone – as he saw the other Arab reaching into his coat. He did not wait to find out why – he picked up a chair and smashed it against the guy, sending him flying. Zelda pulled out a revolver.

Excuse me, she said to the other guy. You are standing in our way.

The man – on closer examination he could have been Egyptian – stared at the gun, looked at her and smiled and said coolly as he moved out of the way, Excuse me...

His companion's mouth was bleeding. As he got up he held a white handkerchief to his face. He said, Your friend was impatient. He could have asked us to step aside.

Zelda said, Come...

They went through a dark passage, climbed the narrow stairs out of the cellar and entered the street. A car was waiting. The back door was open. Herr Hess called from the driving seat,

Quick! Get in!

They jumped in and Hess gunned the car away while they were still closing the car door. The two Arabs appeared in the doorway of the club. They watched the car drive off.

The cool one shook out a Lucky Strike and put it in his mouth. He lit it with a Zippo lighter – inhaled – then the let the smoke trickle out...

In the back of the car Zelda held his hand, tight. Herr Hess drove fast until it became clear they were not being followed. He eased down to cruising speed. She laughed, easing the tension. Her grip on his hand lightened but she still held it,

That was great! By Lenin's beard! What do we do for an encore, darling?

He considered this – whoever he was, did it really make a difference – before answering, What will they do for the encore?

It was not far to the Hotel Herman. Hess stopped the car opposite the entrance. He leant back and opened the rear door for them to alight on to the pavement. Zelda whispered to Hedge, Should we tip the driver?

The couple alighted. Hess shut the door and pulled out into the traffic. Zelda held on to Hedge's arm. She indicated the disappearing Mercedes with the dented right wing and smashed headlight,

Is he a friend of yours?

I don't know.

He's your minder, she said. Of course. I should have guessed.

He killed my previous minder to get the job.

It must pay well, she said brightly.

They entered the Hotel Herman.

Mr Green was getting his oats. It was something that had eluded

Inspector Hedge for some considerable time and all sorts of excuses like pressure of work were quite banal and nobody but himself was listening. Mr Green, on the other hand, was working – he was on the job – and he was not complaining.

Afterwards smoking the post coital cigarette she looked at him for a long moment and said, I noticed you are not circumcised.

Hedge frowned, to concentrate, pushed to make a convincing story. My father was sent to the camps and my mother was not Jewish but...

She interrupted him. George, you don't have to convince me. Your story is not right. You do not have to be Jewish but people will assume so.

You think I should have become circumcised before I took on this work?

Mr Green, we know that you were in Iceland on your way to Norway to purchase twenty tons of Heavy Water for Israel – a consignment that was conveniently surplus to the requirements of the UK Government for whom it was originally intended. Heavy Water is not necessary in using atomic energy for peaceful purposes – so what use can it be intended for? Except for the Bomb?

I've no idea.

Really? How interesting. Yes, we knew you were a replacement Mr Green, darling, because the original Mr Green drowned in a boating accident. He was a Mossad agent so lethal accidents are only to be expected. It is obvious that elements of the British Secret Service are in collusion with Israel. That is why you are here. What we do not know is how many Mr Greens you have in reserve?

I've no idea what you're talking about.

Are you finding another route to Norway? We will stop you. No matter how many Mr Greens you have. And do tell them to ensure that any future Mr Greens are circumcised, won't you? It's details like that which blow your cover.

Zelda Dubrovnik was out of bed and getting dressed.

Are you going?

I'm sorry. I must go.

I see. He watched her. Sheer woman. God's gift to this earth. He said, Through the icy fog of Cold War are you suggesting that I have been seconded to Mossad?

We want to do a deal with your government. By pretending it isn't happening they are helping Israel to develop a nuclear arsenal. We need to stop this – now – while there is still time. Then later we will publicly launch a new initiative – an invitation to the USA to reduce nuclear weapons. The Soviet Union is only interested in Peace. Not war.

I am to carry that message back to my masters, am I? Forgetting the propaganda element. Perhaps you'll invite me to your next Peace Conference.

We are offering to work with you – to put our agencies together to avoid a catastrophe. Is it not better to rescue something good out of this? Is this not the beginning of cooperation? That could lead to a thaw in our relationship – country to country. This is what the Soviet Union desires.

He said, Are you giving me the message? Does Zelda need a receipt? Let's put it his way, is Russia helping Egypt to build an atomic bomb? To balance the equation?

No, George, definitely not. The Soviet Union is definitely against nuclear proliferation. More than ever in the Middle East. How long would a balance of terror last there? Ask yourself that. It would be better that Israel gets the Bomb and denies its existence. But we cannot play that scenario. Not yet....

She leant over and kissed him lightly. I have so much enjoyed tonight, thank you.

You underestimate yourself, George. You are a really nice guy.

Inspector Jack Hedge frowned. Who was the nice guy? Not that discarded label. Really? He replied. Is this reality?

As close as it gets, darling. Let's both come out of this alive. We are only – how do you say – the boots on the ground? She blew him another kiss, opened the door and peered out into the passage. Then she was gone. The door was closed and he was alone. And all that she had been that night went with her – and all hope – but he had not hoped for anything, why start now? A wave of depression hit him. But at least he was back to being a depressed Mr Green, not a depressed Inspector Hedge.

20

At breakfast the next morning Herr Hess was decidedly grumpy. What were you playing at last night, may I ask? I advised you not to leave the hotel. Of course you are not under my orders but if you get bumped off it looks bad for me – I am left with all the explaining to do. And what were you doing with the bitch last night? Apart from the obvious.

I am not answerable to you, Herr Hess. I don't want to make your life difficult but can you pass the marmalade?

Why do you not try these waffles and maple syrup? Since the Occupation breakfast in Berlin has become more interesting. Hess was tucking into the waffles, with fried eggs and crispy bacon added on the plate.

No thanks. Toast and coffee does me nicely.

Have you a hangover?

No. I don't drink much. Never have.

That Zelda Dubrovnik is KGB. Is that not obvious to you. They are the enemy. My God they are here in West Berlin and our agents are in East Berlin, true – so we stay in touch you could say but we must be careful.

Without asking he took a piece of toast from Mr Green's plate and mopped up his egg yolk... Yah, it would have been easier if the Allies had joined with the Wehrmacht in 1945 to fight the Russians – that was the opportunity! Missed! Now we are involved in a war of attrition – of wearing down – of nerves – it is all to do with the nervous state! How long do we go on like this? What that Soviet whore told you is all lies, believe me. You spoiled yourself with her, Mr Green. Go and see a doctor is my advice.

You are recycled Nazi, Herr Hess. Now on the side of Israel, is that it?

I am recycled by US Intelligence, yes. They are running me. I was not involved in the Genocide. My grandfather was Jewish. But my grandmother disowned him to save us saying her husband was not my father's father.

Where did you learn that parlour trick? Commented Hedge née Green.

I am frayed at the edges today, Mr Green. Hess at last had finished with his plate, having wiped it clean. Do you mind if I smoke? It is one of my five cigarettes a day – no more than five.

Go ahead.

Danke.

While Hess lit up, Hedge poured hot water into the teapot and poured himself another cup of tea. I suppose I should thank you for being there when needed last night, Herr Hess.

It is my employment.

Nevertheless, I recognise that I am in your debt. If I can ever repay it?

Yah! We will go for a drive to the suburbs of West Berlin today , Mr Green. It is pleasant. Close to the border with East Germany which is a minefield. It cannot be crossed without the right papers. We are filling in the time, you understand. I have no orders for today. We will conduct ourselves as tourist and guide. I have a generous petrol allowance. Hess paused... Well, I have a small errand to perform which I hope you will not object to. You see, Mr Green, it is Thursday – Donnerstag – it is Mutti's – that is my Mother – it is her Eightieth Birthday today.

Congratulations.

I thought – if you don't mind, Mr Green – that we would call in to see her

Oh. Right. Of course I don't mind.

To see my Mutti.

Anything to oblige. Yes, by all means, let's do something for somebody else for a change – other than play war games. To make your mother happy on her Eightieth Birthday, yes. That is something I am pleased to share with you, Herr Hess. Today.

Danke, Mr Green. Danke. Danke. She is in a home for war widows. They share a belief that keeps them going – an hallucinated belief that Adolph Hitler is in South America plotting the rise of the Fourth Thousand Year Reich. So? What do you think?

21

In the hall of the State Home for Wehrmacht Officers' Widows upon a stage seated on a simple chair sat Adolph Hitler, previously Mr Green, previously Inspector Hedge. Now with a small moustache and hair plastered down across his forehead he wondered was he people pleasing? He hoped not. Was he even convincing? Did it matter to this audience? In the body of the hall were gathered about twenty elderly woman, dressed smartly – though mostly their costumes harked back to the Forties – a few of them bejewelled, those who had managed to hide their valuables from the invading Red Army hordes. Frau Hildegard Hess had pride of place, seated in an ornate chair. Her son, Albert Hess, was addressing the audience,

And it is with true humility and with a sense of immense honour that we welcome our most distinguished guest – who has most secretly come here all the way from South America to meet those who cannot be mentioned you understand, yet still our wonderful Fuhrer found time to pass by and celebrate the Eightieth Birthday of Frau Hildegard Hess. Because of his throat's infection – no alarm please – and his need to save his voice for important matters – Our Beloved Fuhrer has issued a brief statement. He read from a piece of paper...

Women of the The Third Reich, your wombs have served the Master Race, ensuring that future generations will continue to emerge from your prolific reproductions. I thank you for this sacrifice to nature which is serving the Higher Cause of the coming Super Race. Your husbands have known bliss in your arms, Meine Lieben – and your obedience to their commands has been constant and sometimes a little kinky. I thank you from the bottom of my heart that you are remaining loyal to the work of world domination – It is not finished! Let me assure you – I am working with my Generals – and with my scientists – to perfect the miracle weapons – that I have promised – weapons that will overcome all enemies of the Thousand Year Reich! SIEG HIEL!

Those women seated – even those in wheelchairs – rose and raised their right arms in the fascist salute, as they all shouted, SIEG HIEL!

Frau Hildegard Hess, we honour you upon your Eightieth Birthday – rest upon your laurels! May I say on a personal note I do not blame you – it is not your fault that your swine of a husband plotted with the traitorous swinehund, Colonel Staufenberg, to assassinate me! You, Mien Frau, are fortunate to be spared – believe me! Do not tell me that you were not exchanging recipes for strudel with Frau Staufenberg while your husbands were plotting upstairs against me! I add that you are related to the traitor Rudolph Hess who parachuted into England behind my back. Your survival Frau Hess is a miracle of grace from your Fuhrer – but I tell you one more stroke from you or your family and you are out! KAPUT! Enjoy your birthday cake, Frau Hess – it may be your last... SIEG HIEL!

To consternation in the hall and shouts of SIEG HIEL! from bewildered Fraus, the occupants of the stage vacated the boards hurriedly. Frau Hess was in a state of collapse. It might well be her last birthday.

As they drove away from the State Home for Wehrmacht Officers' Widows, Hedge was in a state of shock. What a way to treat your mother on her Eightieth Birthday? He could understand rudimentary German and he could certainly understand unbridled emotion in any language.

That was not the statement we prepared, said Hedge.

Nein. As I was reading it out my eyes blurred, explained Hess.

Blurred?

With tears, yah. I could not see the writing. I had to improvise.

Why were you crying?

It was frustration. That woman has ruined my life. She deserved what the Fuhrer said to her – every word. She cannot blame me. I did not say it.

It was cruel.

Cruel? She dressed me up in frocks when I was a child – she wanted a girl I tell you. Yah. She treated me like one. It was only when I got into the Hitler Youth that I shed the skirts once and for all. It was too late – the damage was done. I hate my Mutti. I cannot have a married life and children – a normal life – to go home at night and put the children to bed and to give my wife my week's wages packet – for reasons I cannot go into now. It is too complicated.

It would have been better if we didn't go. You could have killed her with the shock of your tirade.

Gut. I am a killer. Yah. The son has come home. Now – perhaps – if she survives – she will leave me alone.

Have you tried a psychiatrist?

Psychiatry is a Jewish plot to undermine weak minds. There is no Ego. There is no Id. Have you seen them? There is only the bill to pay for a fantasy treatment. What did the Jew, Freud say? I can only hope to turn misery into everyday unhappiness? What sort of racket is he running? But... Yah, I love my Mutti. Perhaps my words will shock her out of bewilderment.

They passed a sign indicating a slip road ahead leading on to the autobahn and West Berlin. As the Mercedes turned on to it Hess speeded up and they were soon in the heart of Berlin – or was it a heart transplant – anyway it was throbbing even this early in the evening and there they were at the front of the Hotel Herman.

I will pick you up later, said Hess

Why? Where are we going?

You will find out soon enough. About Eleven pm then.

I'm still waiting for my Walther PPK, said Hedge as he alighted the car. I indented for it.

Do you think Mr Green would be armed and dangerous?

Definitely.

OK. See you later.

The Mercedes drove off and Mr Green entered the hotel. The receptionist stared at him as he handed over the room key. Mr Green coughed and removed the Hitler moustache.

22

As he entered the hotel room the phone was ringing.

Hello?

Where the hell have you been, Hedge?

It was his Superintendent.

You've got the wrong room? This is Mr Green speaking.

Very funny, yes. What were you doing all dressed up as Adolph Hitler?

I was at a fancy dress do, Lenny. And for your information I have no mission here, you realise that? I am fishing without bait for old boots.

Well said, Hedge. I'll use that expression. You are on loan to a different agency. They know how to use you.

Then why are you checking up on me? Has the Met got spies in Berlin? How come?

There is a bigger picture...

Well, Lenny, I'm not in any picture so how can I be framed?

You're being clever again, Inspector. I am reminding you of your true identity. One day you will be coming home. Keep that in mind.

The line went to a monotone as the caller hung up. He put the phone down. Whoever he was, he was important enough to be kept under observation. And he, Mr not Miss Green, was still a thread of identity. Male.

In the shower the hot jet of water played upon his body, relaxing him. Was he losing weight? Getting too skinny? Alice, the ex, would have chided him, eat more – have regular meals, Jack – you'll make yourself ill snacking every day – sandwiches – you need vegetables – roughage – fruit – porridge... And then she would disappear for days on end and surface phoning from some drinking club under the pavements of Great Newport Street or – forget it. He stepped out of the shower, reaching for a towel to dry his hair. He put on a luxurious soft white bathrobe which management policy stated he could purchase. What was the use of recalling Alice? Of recycling those memories? Of course memory gifted identity, frustration, regret. Better to stay in the present as Inspector Hedge. Or Mr Green. Or Adolph Hitler...

There was a tap upon the room door. A muffled voice outside called, Room Service! He had ordered nothing. So this was how it was to end? For whoever he was? With mobsters bursting in with silencers on their sub-machine guns or perhaps a simple shotgun held under a bouquet of flowers to deliver a death sentence? This was the end of being Mr Green. But then Mr Green would have lit a cigarette and poured himself a whisky before opening the door and contrived a killing...

He opened the door. It was the bellboy. He held a bunch of a dozen long stemmed white roses. He took them and tipped the kid and closed the door. He read the card tied with a pretty ribbon to the flowers, THANKS FOR A BEAUTIFUL NIGHT!! ZELDA XX. This was the honey trap. Don't fall for it. They were both acting as agents of a foreign power. Spies did not have real emotions, he must keep that in mind. Being Mr Green was living without expectation or regret. He was pretending she was like all the others were – not that he had enjoyed so many love affairs – all he had was the pretence. If he lived it passionately enough could he make it real?

Next problem, go to a philosophy class, discuss the nature of reality.

Could he make it real with Zelda?

Hedge busied himself finding a tall vase and half filling it with water and roughly arranging the roses in it. Don't get too prissy – he wasn't a pooftah – that was still illegal in Britain and his identity crisis had not taken him there though there had been times when...

When he was still a young and pretty policeman he had been put on duty hanging round the Public Lavatories – Leicester Square being a favourite – ensnaring any poor sod who was out for the night cottaging – you're nicked, mate. Come along with me now... And his prepared statement next morning to the court, The accused approached me while I was standing at a urinal stall and asked me if there was anything he could do for me? When I asked him what did he have in mind the accused replied, Anything that makes you happy, as long as it's illegal, darling. Laughter in court. Personally he had not enjoyed that duty nor the joshing that went on back at the Station – You may not be a homo, Jack, but I've heard you help them out when they're busy! He had asked to be taken off that duty which had led to funny looks and even wolf whistles in the canteen. Which way was he swinging?

On the dot of 11pm the phone rang Herr Hess was waiting for him downstairs. He was ready. As he stepped out of the lift into Reception he saw that Herr Hess was chatting up the receptionist. He wondered did his minder like the boys? Was he a two way swinger?

Am I butting in, said Hedge.

Hess turned and smiled widely showing a set of well kept white teeth – presuming they were his because the smile was certainly false. Ah, Mr Green! Good evening! You are ready to roll?

Yes. Do you know where we're going, by any chance?

Of course.

I'm glad somebody does.

With a parting pout at the flashy Something For Everybody Not Quite So Young In A Good Light receptionist, Herr Hess took Hedge by the arm and escorted him from the hotel.

As the Mercedes drove along the West Berlin streets Hedge noticed that floodlights illuminated the many building sites as the work of regeneration continued into the night. Hess in a cheerful mood threw a shoulder holster over into the back seat.

Your shooter! You can sign for it later. You are now armed and dangerous, is that not sexy? He threw over a box of cartridges. Two dozen bullets! Where I come from that meant two dozen bodies! Hess laughed.

He said, If you're killing defenceless civilians I dare say it did.

I have served time, Mr Green, for minor war crimes after being fully investigated. I have nothing to hide except being part of a monstrous past that I could not escape. What do you want to know? Hess sounded hurt. Just when I thought we could be buddies, he added.

I'd rather be buddies with an inflatable doll. They were standard issue at the Yard.

Could you get me one? I would like that.

They were only doing Policewomen Inflatables. Would that be to your taste?

Very definitely take that as yes.

Hedge realised that he had mentioned his background, unnecessarily.

Don't worry, Mr Green, I knew you were a Police Inspector in a previous life. I was briefed. It is in your profile – essential to knowing your psychological makeup – your strengths and your weaknesses. For example did you know that you are classified as a latent homosexual?

Hedge replied, We are all latent everything we are not, Herr Hess.

I agree, Mr Green. Everything moves on fast these days. That is life. The offer of being buddies is still on the table.

He could trust nothing this guy said. Just because he had been to this ex-nazi's Mum's Eightieth Birthday Party dressed as Hitler to return a favour for saving his life did not make him a buddy. After all Hess was employed to save lives as well as to take them. He checked the gun and loaded it. He buckled on the shoulder holster and placed the PPK into it, feeling the weight. It felt good.

They were off the main street and following a minor road which came to some sort of park, shadowed in the darkness. Hess braked the Mercedes opposite a double iron gate, chained and padlocked.

Outside the car Hess said, Please follow me. He went ahead walking alongside a metal linked fence that ran round the property. Hedge followed. Hess was using a torch and eventually found the hole in the fence he was looking for near some bushes.

You go through there, he said. This is where I say goodbye. Someone else will take over. He shone the torch into Hedge's eyes. I should warn you, George, if you are saying things to hurt me I will make sure that you come off worst. Here – take this torch – goodnight. Hess thrust the torch at Hedge, turned and disappeared into the darkness.

Hedge wondered – no, no, it was Mr Green that had to wonder – what the hell was going on in the mind of his minder? Being Mr Green was proving to be an emotional roller-coaster. He managed to climb through the hole in the link fence without snagging his clothes. What was he doing in an out-of-season closed-down funfair? He made for the ghostly shape of the Ferris Wheel which stood out against the moonless night sky. After all that was the place where shady characters could meet – as in the classic film – life often had nothing better to do than to copy cinema.

As he approached the entrance to the ride Margaret stepped out of shadows. She was quietly laughing,

You guessed right, Harry. The Ferris Wheel! It's homage to The Third Man night.

Am I Harry Lime tonight?

Yes, can't you hear the zither? Come on...

She led him on to a carriage and someone unseen started a motor and the wheel began to ascend.

Is MI6 paying for the ride? Or whoever's paying your expenses now?

It's a field exercise. You have to keep the juices running and we couldn't think of anywhere better for a clandestine meeting.

As they rose they watched the lights of Berlin appear – its hopes and fears lay below.

Right, what have you got for us? She asked.

Hedge described his meeting with Zelda Dubrovnik – all that he remembered had passed between them.

Afterwards Margaret commented, We knew she was here in West Berlin. I assume you had sex with Miss Dubrovnik. It's her speciality.

Did Hedge detect a note of jealousy? Was he becoming something of a prize asset?

Do you want a full description?

No thanks, darling. We mustn't get too excited on the job. But do be careful with that woman? She's been trained to use all she's got.

What Hedge had not reported was his trip to the State Home for Officers' Widows. His Super at the Met had demanded a piece of the pie and that was it and anyway why make himself look ridiculous in the eyes of Margaret, obviously his MI5 handler. Why bother to explain to her without looking ridiculous that he had agreed to dress up as Adolph Hitler?

Anything else? She asked. Are we done?

No. We're not done. Why have I got a paranoid fascist as a minder?

No idea, darling. We didn't supply him. He's not one of our blokes.

Then who dug him up?

He's probably CIA. They were good at recycling Nazis after the war. Don't complain to us.

You sent me on this mission.

It's a joint operation, Sweetie. We have to work with the Yanks on this one. They hate sharing Intelligence, as do we. The trouble is – strictly *entre nous* – the CIA are riven at the core. The hardliners are following strict USA Government Policy on non-proliferation of nuclear weapons but the Jewish diaspora is strong there so secretly some in the organisation are doing all they can to help Israel develop the A Bomb – this makes for divisive action on the ground. The right hand not knowing what the left hand is doing.

Hedge said, The right hand is carrying a knife. The Ruskies want us to know that they are against Israel developing the A Bomb. We can work together to stop the Israeli clandestine operation.

Unfortunately it's too late for that, Jack. The Jews are too determined. They see it as vital to the survival of their State which is still only a tiny island in an ocean of hostile Arab countries.

But every Western country is committed to the non-proliferation of Nuclear weapons.

Officially, yes. But unofficially there is more flexibility. For example the French are secretly committed to help Israel get the A bomb. There are over a thousand French boys and girls right now out there in Israel – in the desert – a vibrant community that actually has their mail sent via South America to keep the secret of where they are actually operating.

Do the Soviets know all this?

Yes, of course. Their stance – being so keen to share with us – is a smokescreen. They know it is too late to stop Israel – if ever there was a time when they could have been stopped.

Why are you filling me in on all this? It's not friendly *entre nous* chat is it?

Because we might need to send you to Cairo, Jack. Quite soon. The action is moving there – to Egypt. They know about Israel's nuclear intentions and I tell you the Egyptians are not happy.

I've experienced their unhappiness, Hedge reminded her.

The Met put you in a place of present danger. They were happy to lend you to us. We know why, don't we?

Because the Met are in collusion with the Government to bury my previous case and get me out of the way. And if it's for good and all so much the better. For Christ's sake I met you in that nursing home where incurables were dying off in a top security basement ward, victims of a biological warfare experiment gone wrong. Who are they going to blame when the virus does become totally evident in the community? Bats?

OK, Jack, stop. Obsessing about that won't do you any good. You were drugged-up rotten. Who knows what you imagined as opposed to what was actually going on. Margaret smiled and he remembered how they had met in the grounds of that weird clinic, both as patients apparently. She was talking again...

You are a valuable asset on loan to us. Relax, please. We would love to keep you intact. Moving on to current issues, what the Soviets are doing – or ready to do – or exploring to do – we are not sure – is to help Egypt develop its own nuclear deterrence against Israel.

Hedge digested this piece of information, before saying, The Arabs want to wipe Israel from the face of the earth. Given the A bomb what's to stop them?

Go to the top of the class, dear.

He said, Miss Dubrovnik implied the Russians could switch to another scenario but must appear to be helping Egypt obtain the bomb.

As you mentioned, Jack. And as very much noted, good job. You have been the channel for unofficial information the Russians wanted us to have. You see the value of pillow talk? Is there anything you have forgotten to tell me?

No, that's it.

They looked down upon the lights of West Berlin, a city resurrected from the ruins. At first painfully brick by brick as the buckets were passed hand to hand from the gigantic piles of rubble – until it accelerated into the feat of reconstruction which lay below them today – a coming major economic force to be reckoned with as the giant cranes pecked like mating river birds.

Yet how fragile was the peace upon which it was being built.

Margaret leant over the edge of the carriage and whistled. After a moment the Ferris Wheel creaked, jerked into motion and the big wheel started to turn as they descended back to earth and however many days were granted to them upon it...

23

He had risen late that morning. Inspector Hedge, if that's who he was, sat in the empty dining room of the Hotel Herman drinking coffee. He felt depressed. Instead of being posted to Cairo he had received an envelope with a flight ticket to London, Heathrow, made out to George Green.

Who had sent him the ticket?

Had the Superintendent dissed him? Sent in a report that their man in Berlin had dressed up as Adolph Hitler and had visited German war widows looking for a good time? Was he being returned to normal duties? Or more likely returned to London to be involved in a simple traffic accident? Been done before...

Jack Hedge sipped his coffee considering his options. He did not relish the prospect of his adventures coming to an end. What? Returning to his Earls Court flat and to his thoughts revolving through empty days while she – The Inflatable Policewoman, Doris – bobbed up and down on the settee as he waited for someone somewhere to decide how to get rid of him. One way or another they would bury him and his unfinished case – Code Name Green Swan – that was still rumbling away beneath the foundations of the Establishment in England. It was only a question of time before the virus surfaced and who to blame then?

China?

Perhaps they were planning to send him back to the looney bin in Surrey and pump him up with hallucinatory drugs and turn him into a zombie.

Hello. Are you lost in thought, darling?

It was Zelda Dubrovnik. She sat down. Unaccountably he felt a flood of relief to see her. Was she the enemy? Or his lover come back to play? Or both? He said, I was thinking that I never discovered what messages you were sending from the cottage in the woods.

What cottage? She sat down.

The one with the three bears. Only it was four bears. And you were wearing a yellow dress. Bright yellow! You were on a radio transmitter.

Of course, she said, smiling innocently. I was sending messages of love. They were Top Secret. Don't you think that love is the most clandestine operation in our lives?

I reckon you've been trained in the uses of love.

Every woman learns the uses of love, darling. So what's new?

Would you like some coffee?

Unbidden, the waiter arrived with another cup and a fresh jug of coffee. Hedge poured. Zelda took out a packet of cigarettes.

Do you mind if I smoke?

Yes, I do. Very much. I care for your health.

OK. She smiled radiantly. So you do care. She placed the cigarettes back into her handbag. You don't mind me smoking when it's post-coital, George. Then anything goes. Then I can have my ciggy. Are you in a bad mood today?

I'm being sent back to London to rot.

When?

Tonight. I'm booked on the last flight to London. It's all over you see. I delivered your message, by the way. From your People to my People. I don't think it's going to make a jot of difference. They believe it's all propaganda. Another Peace Initiative.

Can we go to your room, please, George? I have something to show you. It's private.

Why don't you save it for who comes next? Maybe a Mr Brown next time. Or a Mr White.

She stood up. It won't wait. It won't wait for Mr Brown or Mr White. She sipped from her cup and put it down. This coffee is too strong. She stood up...

In the hotel room in bed she smoked her post-coital cigarette. He loved her amazing body, her self-absorption when they had sex.

So? What have you got to show me, Zelda?

I showed you me. All of me, darling, was that not enough for you?

More than enough, thanks. I must not let our love-making become another dependency.

You can depend on your Zelda, darling. Always.

She reached for her handbag. Were you aware that two Arabs saw you as Adolph Hitler? They were very impressed. She took from her bag two photographs of him ridiculously appearing as Adolph Hitler entering the hotel. She handed them to him. It was the second photograph of him not so much in focus that clearly showed two Arabs. The knife Arabs...

Hedge was out of bed, a bathrobe covering his nakedness. Who took these photos?

It does not matter who took the photos. If you are willing to impersonate their idol, the Fuhrer, those probable Egyptians are willing to retreat back into the woodwork. For now.

He was studying the photographs. He handed them back to her, saying, Egypt is relying on Russia for help so I would say you have influence in this matter. It's more likely you that called off those clowns.

Does it matter, darling? She picked up his London air ticket which was on the bedside cabinet. He reached to take it from her,

I'll have my ticket, thank you.

She tore the ticket in two. You do not have to go to London tonight, George.

Oh. He took the torn ticket from her.

She laughed. Don't worry darling, if you do decide it's still a good idea then we will book you a first class seat. Not a miserable economy seat. You see we spend money where it counts and you are valuable to us. She stubbed out her cigarette. Mr Green, we have a proposal of international cooperation between Russia and the West in which you could become most helpful.

No thanks. I'm sure they can reissue this ticket. But I don't mind travelling first class back to London tonight if that's still an offer.

Sure, George, if you are crazy enough, of course. If you go to London they will put you back in the asylum to shut you up. We have your file, Inspector Jack Hedge, plain clothes division. The plain clothes this time will be a white hospital gown with ribbons tied at the back. We know all about your last case, Code Name Green Swan. We have the information. Your country can cooperate with us because the virus will be out soon enough and we already know how lethal it is. But that is another story, darling. Your value is you never do what is expected of you. This quality we appreciate. So who do you want to be? Oh my God – or Lenin – tell me Mr George Green? Inspector Hedge? Adolph Hitler? Which story do you want to tell?

He stared at her. What's on offer?

Darling, you can be helping a new relationship between the Soviet Union and Great Britain. It is time for a thaw in the Cold War. Your cooperation has the blessing of your handler, Margaret.

He tried not to show his surprise. You know Margaret? You mean she has been passing information to Moscow? Had Margaret been turned, was that it? Or was she ever any different? Which meant he had no idea which game he was a pawn in. Zelda Dubrovnik apparently knew everything. She had his MI5 file so someone had passed a copy to her. And she was making him an offer. He could take it or leave it. He could return to London and pick up where he had left off. Memories. Illusions. Hallucinations. Bobbing inflatables...

I need Margaret to confirm what you tell me.

No you do not need Margaret to confirm anything. Margaret is no longer in Berlin. What you need is to make a healthy decision for yourself. You can go back to London, if you please, and be reduced to the state of a vegetable because that is waiting for you. Or you can play a game with us which has its own risks. Such is life.

He said, I need a shower. He moved away but turned at the bathroom door. By the way if I were to play your game? For the sake of international relations, of course. What sort of game did you have in mind?

I can only tell you that, darling, when you agree to take part.

You mean if I agree?

Zelda stretched and lit another cigarette. I don't mean anything, darling. I have given up on meanings. A long time ago...

A private jet took off from Tempelhof Airport heading for an obscure airfield in Argentina. In the main cabin sat Inspector Hedge, née Mr Green, née Adolph Hitler which last he now resembled. Herr Albert Hess sat opposite him. Zelda Dubrovnik came through from the pilot's cabin and down with them.

So... the big adventure begins! You, Mr Green, are the bait. As Adolph Hitler you will be selling your sperm in South America. Well, shall we say sperm – it does not need to be yours.

Thank God. Look, as I am now playing at being Adolph Hitler can we not drop the George Green bit – who is possibly Jewish – and be Jack Hedge? Just between friends?

No, it's better we keep you as George Green. Because in Argentina the Nazis will suspect that you are not Adolph Hitler and that you are Jewish.

But I am not circumcised...

That's a detail. We won't let anyone close enough to check that, don't worry.

Jack Hedge frowned. As long as he knew who he was but how long could he certain of that? He said, I'm not happy about providing sperm for this supposed Thousand Year Third Reich.

She said, unless you want to that won't be necessary. We will have other donors available. In fact aided by a team of doctors you will remain a remote figure. The Nazi war criminals there will be lured out of hiding.

But the sperm is not for them...

No, it will be for their wives, or more likely their mistresses or daughters.

Jack Hedge persevered. But if they suspect that it is all an elaborate hoax – a trap – why would they come?

Because they will suspect it is a sacrilege to their hopes and dreams but they must be sure. They will send someone. Even if they keep a distance and send people to close down what they suspect is a phoney deal still you are the bait to catch the big fish. They will not be able to resist you. They will come. We have studied their psychology.

Zelda Dubrovnik signalled for a pot of coffee and busied herself pouring it for everyone. Inspector Hedge – forever he reminded himself that's who he was though why bother with that scrapbook of memories? He took his coffee black before saying, I see, yes. Well you and your pals have obviously thought this through. I'm looking forward to meeting Martin Boorman and any of the rest of their gang who made it out of the ruins of Berlin. Personally I must say that I prefer this version of reality to anything else on offer...

PS

A MONTH LATER. Somewhere outside Buenos Aires.

Trailing a cloud of dust the Humber Super Snipe drove up the track towards the farmhouse. It parked in the yard and a man and woman alighted. From an outhouse stepped a nurse in white hospital scrubs to greet them. It was Albert Hess. They disappeared into the building.

Wake up! Wake up, George!

Jack Hedge awoke staring into the harsh light of day against which Zelda was framed as she shook him. Get up, she said. Our first couple has arrived.

What?

Yes, she will be having the impregnation now. It will not take long. And you need to be seen at the window as Adolph Hitler.

Not necessary. Jack turned over and pulled the covers up.

Of course it is necessary. That is why we are here. Get up! We must let the news spread. Hitler was glimpsed at the window.

Jack sat up. They will know it is fake. What's the point?

The point is people will believe what they want to believe.

He got up and went to the bathroom. She followed, standing in the doorway as he relieved himself.

Can you believe it? At last our first couple has arrived, George.

It was early, too early in the morning to identify himself as George let alone as Adolph Hitler. She knew he was Jack Hedge, didn't she? But did he know it? His identity was slipping. Inspector Hedge? Mister Plod. He flushed the toilet and yes he did wash his hands and then dowsed his face in cold water. He stared at his reflection...

That stupid moustache is coming off.

Keep it, darling. Or you will have to use a stick-on Hitler moustache. You know that irritates your skin.

He dried his face. Better. That was better. He looked at his Russian princess. She was beautiful. What? Too good for him? No, for he was a Prince come to rescue her from a spell of enchantment. What as? A frog?

109

No, last night it was decided she was a book of regulations and he had turned her back into a magical story...

He said, It would help if you called me Jack.

She brought him a brown shirt. Here, put his on.

He put on the shirt and the Alpine shorts and the socks and shoes with a tassel and didn't he look the part. She combed his hair across his forehead...

Perfect darling. Now go to the window. The medical impregnation procedure does not take long. The couple will be out soon. We hope they see you. As soon as they do you move away from the window. As if they cannot be sure what they have seen. But cannot stop talking about it. Job done.

Jack said, Then I can have a cup of coffee. He kissed her lightly. Got that, Eva?

She laughed. Am I your Eva Braun now, darling? Which game are we playing?

I never stop asking myself that? And more importantly who... ? Who is playing the game?

He moved to the window. A moment later the couple appeared, coming out of the building in what seemed to be a hurry. She climbed into the car. Before he got in he looked up briefly and saw the image of the Fuhrer looking back at him. Jack had scored. He moved away from the window. The man stared at the empty space then got in and a moment later the Humber Super Snipe drove out of the yard and in a cloud of dust disappeared down the track.

In the kitchen Zelda had prepared coffee when Jack, now out of his Tyrollean costume, and minus the Hitler moustache came in. He rubbed his lip,

Sorry. I couldn't bear it a moment longer.

She poured his coffee. She kissed him lightly, I prefer you like that. You are restored to George.

It's a journey, he retorted. We will get to Jack next stop.

She laughed. And then what?

Oblivion, he announced, sipping his coffee appreciatively. By the way where's Albert? Still playing nursey? Jerking off into a test tube to prepare the next batch of Fuhrer sperm?

Albert Hess, who had adapted quickly to the role required of him and had been schooled in the technique of administering artificial insemination, liked his morning coffee break. He loved to talk and remind everyone that he was an ex-Nazi now, loyal and devoted to the Allied cause. Later Zelda and Jack left the farmhouse and crossed the yard to the outhouse converted to an effective medical room to check on Hess. They hoped to catch him masturbating. That would be a laugh. Jack pushed open the door. Herr Albert Hess lay in a pool of blood upon the floor. Jack checked his pulse. There was none. Hess had been stabbed to death. They returned to the house and Zelda made a phone call. Before noon the cleaners had arrived and removed the corpse and tidied up the medical room. After they had departed Jack Hedge asked,

Now what?

Now I am to take over medical duties, darling. Yes, I know how to do it.

And who is to provide the Fuhrer sperm?

Zelda laughed. The cleaners left two fresh samples in the fridge. As instructed.

Their loyalty knows no bounds, replied Jack. Meanwhile we are sitting ducks.

Quack, quack, said Zelda.

Funny, I think not. Jack was not smiling. I mean sitting ducks soon become dead ducks. We were told to expect a queue of gullible couples turning up to give birth to a Glorious Fourth Reich before the top Nazis in hiding sent in their goons. Did we expect Martin Boorman to personally come and sort us out?

We are not paid to think, darling.

I am paid to solve crimes. That's my job. I am paid to prevent crime and to keep the peace.

Well darling, expecting you to keep the peace in Argentina is a big ask, don't you agree? Zelda placed a cigarette in a holder and lit up, gratefully drawing in the smoke.

Jack, clinging to the wreckage, squeezed his eyes and rubbed his face before he continued. I can't disagree with that proposition Zelda. Listen, there won't be any long queues for Fuhrer sperm. Before that someone will be coming for us. They will close our operation down double quick.

That's better for us darling, yes. This morning's charming sperm seekers may already be leading our people back to the big fish. The Comrades are watching our backs, don't worry.

They didn't watch out for Herr Hess.

He was a Nazi bastard. Nephew to Rudolph Hess. He was dispensable.

What makes you think we are not dispensable? Suggested Jack. True he was off his turf, on assignment so to speak, but he had signed a contract and the same principles of service applied. Except that they did not. They were as dispensable as anything or anyone else. The truth was he had been sent here to die. It was the most convenient way to get rid of him. It was the endgame of his previous case which nobody Upstairs in Q or any other letter of the alphabet wanted him to solve. An un-named virus was out in the community and no-one could stop it now. He stared at Zelda. Nothing seemed to disturb her calm. He said, They're coming to get us, aren't they? It's a matter of hours.

Zelda smiled. So...?

So we run.

Jack thought, she won't run. She can't. Her mind won't let her. She has been hopelessly indoctrinated.

OK, she said. She stubbed out the cigarette. Give me five minutes. I need to get a few things together. Zelda left the room. He was wrong. They would run...

They would run. Together. Because that's what they did. She would be armed and dangerous. Bullets and tampons, that's all she needed. He would travel light. He was rid of the burden of being Adolph Hitler. Rid of the weight of being George Green. Rid at last of being Inspector Hedge. He would be of the moment. Running. With her. Because that's what they did. They would run. They would make love. They were of the moment. Of the wind and rain. Of the sun the moon and stars. Of the river to the sea. Of the next breath, until...

Call me Jack.

www.ingramcontent.com/pod-product-compliance
Lightning Source LLC
Chambersburg PA
CBHW050412030726
47503CB00006B/2152